7214   7738

FRESH INK

EDITED BY LAMAR GILES,
cofounder of WE NEED DIVERSE BOOKS

Crown ♛ New York

Compilation copyright © 2018 by We Need Diverse Books

Foreword copyright © 2018 by Lamar Giles • "Eraser Tattoo" copyright © 2018 by Jason Reynolds • "Meet Cute" copyright © 2018 by Malinda Lo • "Don't Pass Me By" copyright © 2018 by Eric Gansworth • "Be Cool for Once" copyright © 2018 by Aminah Mae Safi • "Why I Learned to Cook" copyright © 2018 by Sara Farizan • "A Stranger at the Bochinche" copyright © 2018 by Daniel José Older • "A Boy's Duty" copyright © 2018 by Sharon G. Flake • "One Voice: A Something In-Between Story" copyright © 2018 by Melissa de la Cruz • "Paladin/Samurai" text copyright © 2018 by Gene Luen Yang, art copyright © 2018 by Thien Pham • "Catch, Pull, Drive" copyright © 2018 by Schuyler Bailar • "Super Human" copyright © 2018 by Nicola Yoon

All rights reserved. Published in the United States by Crown Books for Young Readers, an imprint of Random House Children's Books, a division of Penguin Random House LLC, New York.

Crown and the colophon are registered trademarks of Penguin Random House LLC.

"Tags" copyright © 2013 by Walter Dean Myers used by permission of HarperCollins Publishers

Visit us on the Web! GetUnderlined.com

Educators and librarians, for a variety of teaching tools, visit us at RHTeachersLibrarians.com

Library of Congress Cataloging-in-Publication Data
Names: Giles, L. R. (Lamar R.), editor.
Title: Fresh ink / edited by Lamar Giles, cofounder of We Need Diverse Books.
Description: First edition. | New York : Crown, 2018. | Summary: "An anthology featuring award-winning diverse authors about diverse characters. Short stories, a graphic novel, and a one-act play explore such topics as gentrification, acceptance, untimely death, coming out, and poverty, and range in genre from contemporary realistic fiction to adventure and romance"—Provided by publisher.
Identifiers: LCCN 2018006762 (print) | LCCN 2018021487 (ebook) | ISBN 978-1-5247-6630-6 (ebook) | ISBN 978-1-5247-6628-3 (hardback) | ISBN 978-1-5247-6629-0 (glb)
Subjects: LCSH: Short stories, American. | CYAC: Short stories.
Classification: LCC PZ5 (ebook) | LCC PZ5 .F88 2018 (print) | DDC [Fic]—dc23

Printed in the United States of America
10 9 8 7 6 5 4 3 2 1
First Edition

In memory of
Walter Dean Myers

CONTENTS

FOREWORD

Dear Reader,

When I was a teenager, I *hated* reading.

Well, not *hate* hate. *Love* hate. Me and reading, we had our issues.

I was still the guy who'd asked my mom for a new book every time we stepped into a store. Still the guy who, at age eleven, read Stephen King's *It* in a week and decided I wanted to write (despite being sleep-deprived from terror and never wanting to see a clown again). Still the guy who escaped into fictional worlds every chance I got because they were better than dealing with my mean peers, or my mean stepdad, or the mean real world. In books, *mean* didn't beat the hero. That was everything to me. For a while.

What changed? It became pretty freaking clear that, book after book, adventure after adventure, the heroes weren't like me at all. I don't mean short and moderately athletic with severe seasonal allergies, because I'm aware those traits might hinder one's ability to save the city/world/galaxy. I mean black boys. More often than not, if I ran across a character who shared my race and gender in a book he was a gross stereotype, comic relief, token sidekick, or, depending on genre (I'm looking at you, science fiction, fantasy, and horror), there to die so the real hero could fight another day. This was not an uncommon problem.

Any of my friends who didn't fit a certain mold had the same issue. Finding ourselves in the stories we loved was hard, frustrating work. But when we discovered that rare story that reflected us, that hidden gem, we latched on and fell in *LOVE love* with reading all over again. For some of us in that renewed state of romantic bliss, we made vows to write the stories we had such a hard time finding.

With the book that you hold in your hands, *we've un-hidden the gems!* In these pages are all sorts of heroes. There's one who doesn't speak but flies around with a jet pack to fight monsters. One who's nervous about bringing her girlfriend to family dinner. One who outswims ignorance as well as his competitors. And more. I hope you find one who looks like you, or thinks like you, or *feels* like you. If not, I hope you find glimpses into other worlds that are both respectful and enlightening. Whatever your experience among these pages, know this about the twelve stories collected here: they're presented with nothing but love.

Lamar Giles

ERASER TATTOO

by Jason Reynolds

Shay's father climbed up into the driver's seat of a rental truck and slammed the door. Started the engine, cut the emergency blinkers, then honked the horn twice to say goodbye, before pulling off. Moments later, another truck pulled up to the same spot—a replacement. Double-parked, killed the engine, toggled the emergency blinkers, rolled the windows up until there was only a sliver of space for air to slip through.

"What I wanna know is, why you get to give me one, but I can't give you one?" Dante asked, leaning forward, elbows resting on his knees, his eyes on the street as the people in the new truck—a young man and woman—finally jumped out, lifted the door in the back, studied whatever was inside. Brooklyn was being its usual self. Alive, full of sounds and smells. A car alarm whining down the block. An old lady sitting at a window, blowing cigarette smoke.

The scrape and screech of bus brakes every fifteen minutes. A normal day for Brooklyn. But for Shay and Dante, not a normal day at all.

"Oh, simple. Two reasons. The first is that I can't risk getting some kind of nasty eraser infection. I'm too cute for that. And the second is that my dad will come back, find you, and kill you for marking me," Shay replied, stretching her arms over her head, then sitting back down on the stoop beside Dante.

"Kill me? Please. Your pops *loves* me," Dante shot back confidently. He wiped sweat from his neck, then snatched the pencil he had tucked behind his ear and gave it to Shay. They had been planning this ever since she got the news— ever since she told him she was leaving.

"Um . . . 'love' is a strong word. He *likes* you. Sometimes. But he *loves* me." Shay pushed her finger into her own sternum, like pushing a button to turn her heart on. Or off.

"Not like I do." Dante let those words slip from his lips effortlessly, like breathing. He'd told Shay that he loved her a long time ago, back when they were five years old and she taught him how to tie his shoes. Before then, he'd just tuck in the laces until they worked their way up the sides, slowly crawling out like worms from wet soil, which would almost always lead to Dante tripping over them, scraping his knees, floor or ground burning holes in his denim. Mrs. Davis, their teacher, would clean the wounds, apply the Band-Aid that would stay put only until school was over. Then Dante would slowly peel it off because Shay always needed to see it, white where brown used to be, a blood-speckled boo-boo waiting to be blown. Kissed.

• • •

Shay smiled and bumped against Dante before turning to him and softly cupping his jaws with one hand, smushing his cheeks until his lips puckered into a fish face. She pressed her mouth to his for a kiss, and exaggerated the suction noise because she loved how kissing sounded—like something sticking together, then coming unstuck.

"Don't try to get out of this, Dante," she scolded, releasing his face. "Gimme your arm." She grabbed him by the wrist, yanked his arm straight. Then she flipped the pencil point-side up and started rubbing the eraser against his skin.

They'd been sitting on the stoop for a while, watching cars pull out and new cars pull in. Witnessing the neighborhood rearrange itself. They'd been sitting there since Dante helped Shay's father carry the couch down and load it into the truck. The couch was last and it came after the mattresses, dressers, and boxes with SHOES or BOOKS or SHAY'S MISC. in slanted cursive, scribbled in black marker across the tops. Up and down the steps Dante had gone, back and forth, lifting, carrying, moving, packing, while Shay and her mother continued taping boxes and bagging trash, pausing occasionally for moments of sadness.

Well, Shay's mother did, at least. She couldn't stop crying. This had been her home for over twenty years. This small, two-bedroom, third-floor walk-up with good sunlight and hardwood floors. A show fireplace and ornate molding. Ugly prewar bathroom tiles, like standing on a psychedelic chessboard. This was where Shay took her first steps. Where she took sink baths before pretending her dolls were mermaids in the big tub. Where she scribbled her name on the wall in her room under the window, before slinking into her parents' bed to snuggle. This was where she left trails of stickiness across the floor whenever coming inside with a Popsicle from the ice-cream truck. Where she learned to water her mother's plants. Plants they weren't able to keep because now this space—their space—was gone. Bought out from under them. Empty. All packed into a clunky truck that was already headed south. And since Shay's father left early to get a jump on traffic, it seemed like a good idea to let her mother take a much-needed moment to weep in peace.

Plus, then Shay could have a much-needed moment to eraser-tattoo Dante.

• • •

It felt like nothing at first, to Dante. No different than a finger rubbing.

"Where y'all goin' again?" Dante asked.

"For the *millionth* time, Dante, North Carolina."

"I know that part. I mean, what city?" Dante's skin started to itch a bit.

"Wilmington," Shay said. "Not too far from the water."

Dante didn't say anything. He had never heard of

Wilmington, so he figured it was far. Figured it was a place buses couldn't get to.

"And that's good. I mean, not good that I have to move but that I'm gonna be near water so I can work on my career stuff. Maybe get an internship or something."

"I know, Shay. You wanna save fish and whales and all that."

One of the new tenants, a young white woman, came from the truck and approached the house, her wavy hair whipping in the breeze. She climbed the steps carrying a chair over her head. Dante scooted to the left an inch to let her by.

Shay cocked her head to the side, lifted the pencil for a moment, the air instantly cooling Dante's arm. "A marine biologist. Somebody gotta care for all the stuff underwater that nobody can see. It's a beautiful world down there, full of living things that most folks don't understand."

"Like sharks."

"Like fish that glow in the dark."

Dante ticked his tongue against his teeth. "Fish that glow, Shay? *Really?*" He shook his head. "It don't matter anyway, because when I get rich and famous for building bridges, I'm gonna build one from here to . . ."

"Wilmington."

"Wilmington."

"Or, you could just buy me a plane ticket." Shay chuckled to herself and started in again with the eraser. She was concentrating on the top of the *S*, a curved back-and-forth motion—a frown.

"I'm gonna buy you a plane ticket. Shoot, I might just buy you a whole plane. *And* this house so we can live in it."

Shay nodded but didn't respond.

"You don't believe me?"

"I do. I just don't want to think about all that." Shay glanced up at him with sadness, a dim shooting star in her eyes. She blinked it away. "Right now, I just want to think about burning my initial into your arm."

"Yeah . . . and, just so you know . . . um . . . it's starting to burn."

"Am I not worth the pain?" Shay tightened her face, cut her eyes at Dante playfully.

"Whatever, Shay. Ain't like you getting *my* initial. So don't give me that."

"Come on, Dante. Let's be real—"

Just then, she was interrupted, not by Dante, or by any sound. Just by the other new tenant—the white man from the truck, cradling a big box, waddling up the stoop. Dante scooted a little more to the left, this time to let the guy pass before he was bowled over.

Shay picked up her thought. "Let's be real," she said. "What if we break up?" And before Dante could interject with all the reasons they wouldn't, and *why would you even think like that,* Shay added, "Not that we will or that I want that, because I don't. But . . . what if we do? Then I gotta have that ugly *D* on my arm forever."

"And I'm gonna have this *S,* so . . ."

"Yeah, but at least you'll be able to tell people it's a snake or something. What am I gonna say?"

"Whatever, Shay." Dante winced as the eraser broke the skin, and the two people trotted past them, back down the steps. Back to the truck.

"Hurt?" Shay asked slyly.

"A little," Dante lied. It hurt like hell. Like someone was trying to strike a match on his flesh. He glanced down at his arm, the eraser rolling back the brown as Shay started on the curve.

"You don't gotta lie. Remember who you talkin' to. The girl who healed your boo-boos when we were kids."

"Uh-huh. Which is why this is so funny—the girl who taught me how to tie my shoes so I wouldn't hurt myself is now . . . hurting me," Dante said, through his teeth.

"Ah, so it *does* hurt."

"It hurts, Shay. It hurts. It didn't at first, but now it does."

"Just don't think about it. Take your mind off of it."

"Um . . . I can't. I mean, what you want me to think about? I can't think of nothing except for the fact that my arm's on fire!" Dante now clinched his jaw and squirmed on the rough clay step. He was doing his best not to quit, to keep his word and go through with this even though he was regretting it more and more each second.

"Okay, okay." Shay stared up at the sky, thinking. "How 'bout . . . You remember when you told me you loved me?"

"The first time?"

"No. We were five. That ain't count. You told *everybody* you loved them back then. You used to kiss your juice boxes after you drank them and tell the straw the same thing." Shay shook her head.

"I did love juice boxes, though." Dante shrugged. "Seriously, straws are *made* for kissing!"

"Whatever." Shay shook her head again. "I'm talking about the first time you told me *forreal*. In the ninth grade."

A smile crept onto Dante's face. A perforated smile, interrupted every few seconds by a grimace. Partly due to the burn from the eraser, partly due to the burn from the memory. "Yeah. It was part of our secret handshake at first. Two claps, a pound, one clap, a dap, then '*I love you*' from the both of us."

"Exactly, and we had been friends so long that it was no big deal. Like family. Until one day . . ." She was scrubbing his skin vigorously with the eraser, now coming into the second curve. Almost done.

"Until . . ." Dante's words caught in his throat, overtaken by a painful hiss. "Until one day I hit you with the smooth okey-doke."

"Wasn't no damn okey-doke!" Shay teased. "You dapped me, and we both said 'I love you,' like usual, except you wouldn't let go. And you had this wild look in your eye like my face was lunch or something."

"Yeahhhhhh." Dante gave a cocky nod.

"No, Dante. It was scary. But then you said it again. But you were super serious. Like real serious."

"And you remember what you said?" Dante bit his lip to hold in a grunt. Again, part eraser, part memory.

"You always try to bring that up."

"No, Shay, *you* brought this whole thing up! I just wanna make sure before you move to Willington—"

"Wilmington."

"Whatever. I just wanna make sure before you move you get this part of the story straight. So, I told you I loved you, but this time I said it forreal. And *you* said . . ."

Shay sighed. "And I said, '*No doubt, homie.*'"

"NO DOUBT, HOMIE!" Dante yelped, showering Shay in fake disappointment. "That's what you said!" Dante dramatically slapped his free hand to his chest. When the *"no doubt, homie"* fiasco first took place, he thought his heart would split in half. But it'd been a long time and he'd gotten over it, for the most part. Now it was just something he loved to tease Shay about.

"Because I didn't think you were serious!"

"But you just said you *knew* I was serious, Shay!"

"Okay. Okay. So, I was scared. Because I knew I loved you too, but it was strange. It's always been me and you, and so for you to, like, try to make it *us,* well, that was a little weird for me at first. But after we walked away from each other, what happened?"

"Well, I was *crushed.*"

"No you weren't!"

"Oh, yes I was. But then you ran up behind me and pinched me on the butt, and I knew you loved me too."

"*Yeahhhhhh!*" Shay howled. "And that is what you call game."

Dante shook his head, first at Shay, then at the young man and woman now carrying a mattress toward them. They started up the stoop, but Dante and Shay had no more space to scoot over. They were already up against the railing.

Dante put his free hand up. "Wait, wait, we can just

get off the stoop so y'all can go up," he snapped, his tone somewhere between annoyed and confused. He and Shay stepped down so the couple could step up. "I just don't know why they couldn't say excuse me," Dante grumbled, loud enough for the couple to hear. But they didn't respond. Didn't even flinch. And as Shay and Dante watched the man and woman struggle up the steps inside, they also watched Shay's mother struggle down the steps, eventually bumbling through the front door.

"Wasn't even out of the house before they started moving in all their shit," Shay's mother muttered under her breath. She wiped her eyes, then glanced up, noticing Shay and Dante at the bottom of the stoop. She flashed a sad grin. One of loss and love. One of understanding. "You ready, baby?"

Shay nodded, sighed. Her mother moved slowly, as if giving each foot a moment to mourn each step, and Shay threw her arms around Dante, kissing him on the cheek.

"I love you." It slipped easily from his lips. Like breathing. Like usual.

"No doubt, homie," she replied, her whisper bookended by sniffles. Then she pinched him on the butt.

Dante walked Shay and her mother to the car, opened the passenger-side door. Before Shay got in, she gingerly put the pencil back behind Dante's ear, and he held his arm out so she could see her work. She blew on it, her breath cooling the burn for just a moment.

"Looks good," she said, simply, while slipping down into the seat.

"Not exactly." Dante forced a smile, closed the door, and told Shay to call him when she got there. To Wilmington. A place he'd never heard of, where buses probably didn't go. He watched Shay and her mother pull away, their car easing slowly past the double-parked truck—its emergency blinkers still on—that had left only a sliver of space to get through. And as they turned the corner, vanishing from sight, Dante glanced down at the *S* on his arm again. The burn. White where brown used to be.

He knew the sting wouldn't last forever.

But the scar would.

MEET CUTE

by Malinda Lo

Agent Dana Scully was not in a good mood.

Nic watched surreptitiously as the black girl in the red wig and black pantsuit, FBI badge clasped to the lapel, got in line behind her. She was scowling at her cell phone and texting furiously. When she finished her message, she pocketed her phone and crossed her arms, irritated frown still in place as she looked over the crowd. The line for the preview screening of *Queen of the East*—one of the biggest events at the Denver Science Fiction and Fantasy Convention—was rapidly filling the lobby in front of the Rocky Mountain Ballroom. Nic spotted a Star Wars Rebel Alliance group, two Minions, and a bunch of people dressed as the Queen of the East herself, in her gold leggings, shiny black trench, and silver hair. The multistory lobby echoed with the sounds of excited chatter about the upcoming preview.

Nic eyed Scully. "Did Mulder piss you off or something?"

14

Scully's gaze jerked to Nic. "What?" she snapped.

Nic held up her hands. "Sorry! I just—you seemed upset."

"Upset?" Scully repeated, her lip curling. "Who are you?" Her eyes swept Nic up and down in a decidedly judgmental manner that made Nic flinch.

"I'm—"

"Gender-flipped Sulu?" Scully said.

Nic was surprised. "Yeah! How did you know?"

Scully gestured to the Starfleet insignia on Nic's shirt. "It's not rocket science. And there's only one Asian on *Star Trek*."

Nic frowned. "Yeah. Well." Scully was unexpectedly hostile for a DenCon cosplayer. Nic turned away, feeling uncomfortably insulted, and glanced at the group of guys ahead of her in line. They were dressed as zombies, which indicated a distinct lack of creativity, but at least none of them were angry at her for no reason. One of them nodded at her.

"Yo, Sulu," he said. He did a double take. "Wait, you're a girl. How does that work?"

Nic's mood, already soured, went further south. "How does your mouth work when it's dripping with that bloody drool?"

The zombie, whose face was painted with gross, slimy makeup, looked startled.

"I hate it when girls think they can cosplay men," one of the other zombies said. He had a glistening trail of drool on his chin. "It always looks so lame."

"I hate it when guys think slapping on fake blood and plastic wounds equals anything remotely cool," Scully said. "And stop insulting disabled people."

The zombies blinked in unison. "Dude," drool-face zombie said, shaking his head. "Somebody's on the rag."

Scully gave him a smile so sharp it made Nic think of a shark baring its teeth. "Aw, are you afraid of bleeding women? Not sure how you'll survive as a zombie."

Nic stifled a laugh while the guys gaped at Scully. They shuffled together, their egos clearly deflated, and turned their backs in a huff. Nic realized they were probably in high school, like her, hiding their pimply faces beneath all that zombie makeup. They were no match for poised and sweetly vicious putdowns from a pretty girl.

"That was awesome," Nic said to Scully.

"I'm tired of assholes." Her expression softened slightly. "Sorry if I acted like one."

"No, you didn't. I made a bad joke. Sorry."

Scully shrugged. "No, it was a good joke. Mulder did piss me off."

"What?" Nic said, laughing. "Did you come with a Mulder?"

"I came with a Mulder and a Krycek," she said, rolling her eyes. "But they're a couple and I'm tired of being the third wheel. So I decided to come see this preview without them."

"There is so much meta going on in what you just said, I can't even," Nic said.

Scully grinned. "Yeah. Well, Mulder's real name is Casey, and Krycek's real name is Sebastian, and they've only been together for like three weeks, so they're totally into each other.

We came up with our cosplay as a trio. Seb is Latino, so he and I are both race-bending our characters. See, we even did our IDs." She detached her FBI badge and showed Nic the photo. She had pasted a small picture of herself in costume above the FBI seal identifying her as Special Agent Dana Scully.

"Nice," Nic said. "What's your real name?"

"Tamia. How about you?"

"Nic."

"You're not wearing a wig," Tamia observed.

Nic touched her gelled hair. "Um, no."

"That's some commitment there."

"Nah, this is just my regular hair. I did buy some super-strength gel, though. Like, if you watch the recent movies, John Cho's hair never moves."

"Do you like his version of Sulu better than George Takei's?"

"Well, I like them both. I thought it was cool that they made John Cho's Sulu gay."

"Did you hear that George Takei didn't like it?"

"Yeah. But I think it's about time, and I'm happy that Sulu got to be the gay character. It's too bad there can be only one, though, even in the *Star Trek* universe."

"He got to have a gay Asian husband."

"With no lines," Nic pointed out. "But it's fine. I'm glad he exists. It would be nice if they ever had a queer female character, though."

Tamia didn't answer at first, and Nic wondered if Tamia

was about to ask her a personal question, but then Tamia nodded. "Yeah, totally."

Nic gave Tamia a closer look. She was cute, definitely, with round cheeks and a soft mouth that didn't resemble actual Dana Scully's very much, but she certainly had Scully's self-confidence. Tamia returned her gaze directly, her lips curving up a little.

"What?" Tamia asked.

Caught. "N-nothing," Nic stammered. She hoped she wasn't turning red. That was the problem with being Asian; every tiny blush showed up on her face. "Um, I'm psyched for this movie, *Queen of the East*. Have you read the comics it's based on?" The comic book series was about a female detective in a futuristic Shanghai who tracked down supernatural serial killers.

"No, I only saw the trailer. I'm really glad they cast Asian American actors. I was worried Hollywood would be shitty as usual."

Nic nodded. "Yeah. I can't wait to see it. I really like the actress they cast as the lead too. Have you heard the big spoiler?"

Tamia held up a hand. "No, don't tell me! I don't want to know. I love Alexa Chen. She was so great on *Dark Night*."

"Totally agree." Trying to sound casual, Nic added, "She's really hot."

Tamia's eyebrows rose slightly, and her smile broadened. "Yeah, so—"

The fluorescent lights overhead flickered and went out

with a popping sound, plunging the lobby into darkness. Only the exit signs over the doors remained lit. For a moment, all conversation ceased. Then everyone started talking at once.

"What the hell?" Nic said.

"What's going on?" Tamia asked.

Someone pushed open a set of double doors, letting in dull light from the corridor outside. Through the doorway, rain lashed the floor-to-ceiling windows that lined the exterior of the convention center.

Everyone was pulling out their cell phones, creating a sea of bobbing lights in the cavernous space. One of the zombies complained, "The Wi-Fi died."

Nic checked her phone too. "I don't have any bars. I bet the storm is interfering with reception." Many people, including Tamia, were trying to make calls or send texts. "My brother works in the convention center control room," Nic said to Tamia. "They have emergency procedures and generators and stuff. There'll probably be an announcement any second explaining what happened."

"I hope so," Tamia said, sounding skeptical.

They waited, the minutes ticking by slowly, while rumors began to trickle down the line. "The lightning storm downed power lines" was the first, followed by "Power is out across metro Denver" and "The generators won't start either."

"This is bullshit, man," drool-face zombie complained.

"Somebody needs to tell us what happened!" said one of the Queens of the East in a penetrating but thin voice.

"Calm down, it's going to be fine," a Star Wars Rebel answered.

"Oh my God, someone just fainted!" a person shrieked from across the hall. The crowd turned all at once, like a swarm of bees twisting in midair. The hum of voices—concerned, anxious, frightened—rose in a wave.

Nic was beginning to sweat uncomfortably beneath her polyester *Star Trek* uniform. She plucked at the mustard-yellow fabric, fanning herself in the stuffy air. "Crap," she muttered. "Did the air go off?"

"The air?" Tamia hissed. "You mean we're going to suffocate in here?"

"No," Nic said quickly. "Don't worry. That's not what I meant. Just—you know, the AC units are electric powered too."

"That's supposed to help?" Tamia said, agitated.

The previously orderly line was breaking up into jittery clumps of costumed con-goers. Batmen and Wonder Women, gangs of zombies and squads of Minions, all peering into the cell phone–lit dimness, talking over each other as rumor after rumor flitted through the air.

Nic frowned. "I should go find my brother."

"You know where he is?" Tamia asked.

"I think the control room is near registration," Nic said. She didn't add that the convention center was an impenetrable maze even when the lights were on, or that she'd never before visited her brother in his office.

"These people are beginning to freak," Tamia said, shaking her head. "Look at them! They're a mess."

The collective anxiety was catching. Nic felt it crawling over her skin in a disturbing electric buzz. She didn't care so much about the lights, but being engulfed by a nervous crowd set off her claustrophobia. "I have to get out of here," Nic said. She began to move toward the exit, pushing through the caped Batmen.

Tamia followed her. "Wait, I want to go with you. Besides, it's dark out there and you need some light." Tamia pulled a flashlight from her back pocket.

Nic gaped at her. "You have a flashlight?"

Tamia cocked her head as if Nic were being dense. "Agent Scully does."

Nic shook her head in wonder. "Okay, let's go."

• • •

The exhibit halls of the Rocky Mountain Convention Center were connected by seemingly endless corridors of polished floors lined with multistory glass windows. On a clear day the windows provided beautiful views of the Rocky Mountains, but today the charcoal clouds and drenching rain turned the outdoors into a hellscape that Tamia imagined would be right at home in an apocalypse. Lightning cut a jagged arc across the sky as she and Nic wove their way through the mobs of con-goers. The bright white flash lit everyone's faces for a fraction of a second: eyes wide, mouths open, staring at the storm outside.

A thunderclap shook the floor.

"Come on," Nic said, grabbing Tamia's arm.

Tamia let Nic pull her through the crowd. It was like squeezing through the packed convention floor on opening day, except nobody looked happy to be there. A woman started shouting, "Sarah! Where are you? Sarah!" As the frightened woman came closer, she pushed aside everyone in her path. Tamia and Nic were shoved toward the interior wall, and someone elbowed Tamia in the back.

"Ow!" Tamia said indignantly. She caught only a glimpse of the person who had bumped into her—he was in a grayish-green blob-like suit, with stiff, wiry hairs protruding from the edges—before Nic dragged her through an unmarked door and slammed it shut.

The sound of the crowd outside was instantly muffled. Nic's rapid breathing filled the dark space.

"Are you okay?" Tamia asked.

"I'm fine," Nic said, taking a slower, deep breath. "I just don't like crowds."

"I don't blame you," Tamia said. She swept the flashlight around them. "No crowds here." They were in what looked like a maintenance corridor. The floor was no longer polished tile; it was plain old concrete. Pipes and vents hung from the low ceiling, and the walls were lined with closed doors. The still, dark hallway reminded Tamia of a zillion scenes in *The X-Files*—right before Mulder or Scully barged through a door and discovered something gruesome.

"Why hasn't there been some kind of announcement?" Tamia asked.

"The PA system probably runs on electricity too," Nic said.

"They don't have an emergency generator?" Tamia went to the door they had just come through.

"I can't go back out there," Nic objected. "People are still freaking—I can hear them."

Tamia rattled the handle. "It's locked anyway. We're stuck in here." The maintenance corridor suddenly felt a lot creepier than it had before she realized she couldn't turn right around and leave.

"There's only one way to go, then," Nic said.

Tamia shined the flashlight down the hallway. The beam didn't reach the end.

Nic started walking.

Tamia followed, uncomfortably aware of the dark that crept up behind her. She wished she hadn't watched so many *X-Files* episodes to research her costume. Now she kept imagining Eugene Tooms squeezing through one of those pipes, or tanks full of alien hybrid creatures lurking behind one of those doors, which Nic was about to open—

"It's locked," Nic said, disappointed.

Tamia exhaled.

"There has to be a way out of here," Nic said, continuing down the hall.

Nic tried door after door, but they were all locked. The longer they walked, the quieter it became, until only their footsteps sounded in the low-ceilinged hallway. When Tamia glanced back, she could barely make out the light beneath the door they had come through. The undercurrent of anxiety in her began to intensify. She didn't like being trapped in the dark.

"Hey, look—there's another hallway branching off here," Nic said.

Tamia swung her flashlight in the direction Nic was pointing. The hallway was pitch-black, and the flashlight beam didn't make it very far. "I have a bad feeling about this," Tamia muttered.

Nic laughed, and the sound echoed eerily in the long dark hallway. She stopped laughing. "I have a bad feeling about this too. Let's not go there."

They continued down the main corridor.

"Did you know they used that line in every single Star Wars movie?" Tamia said. She immediately felt like a complete nerd and wished she hadn't brought it up.

"Really?"

"Yeah." Trying to distract herself from worrying they would never escape from this endless maintenance corridor, Tamia continued, "Slightly different usage every time, but it's in every movie, even the new ones. Han Solo says it the most."

"I thought about doing gender-flipped Han Solo."

"I saw this great cosplay photo of that online!"

"Yeah, people do it all the time. That's why I decided to go with Sulu instead. But a lot of people don't get it."

"Really? They should. It's a great costume."

"Thanks."

Nic was reaching for the handle of another door when a crash sounded behind them. They both spun around, Tamia's flashlight sweeping across the floor.

"Was that a door?" Nic asked.

"It sounded like it," Tamia said.

A faint sound drifted toward them from beyond the end of the flashlight beam: a shuffle or a slide, like dragging footsteps. They instinctively moved closer together, shoulders touching. The flashlight flickered, the bulb making a tiny *snick* sound.

"Someone else is in here," Nic whispered.

The footsteps were odd, though. They squelched irregularly across the floor, like rain-soaked sneakers worn by someone with a limp.

The flashlight went out.

Tamia squeaked. She shook the flashlight, but nothing happened. The darkness seemed to rush toward her, a thick, suffocating fog that slid inside her with every shallow breath.

The footsteps kept coming.

Tamia had to get out. If she was trapped in this pitch-black nothingness for a moment longer, she would completely freak, and—

The glow of Nic's cell phone startled her out of her growing panic. "Batteries died?" Nic said.

Tamia shoved her useless flashlight into her pocket and said, "Let's go."

"But what about whoever's back there?"

"They can find their own way." Tamia grabbed Nic's hand and marched her down the corridor away from the squelching footsteps.

They soon came to a branch in the corridor; to the left

a short hallway seemed to end in a set of double doors, and beneath the doors was a dim crack of light. They hurried down the short hall and pushed at the doors together. To Tamia's shock, the doors opened. She and Nic plunged onto a deserted concourse lined with glass windows, still pelted with rain. The doors slammed shut behind them. Tamia spun back, reaching for the handle, but there wasn't one. The doors only opened from the other side.

Nic didn't seem to have noticed. She was looking at their hands, still clasped together. They both let go.

Nic turned away and said, "We must be on the other side of the convention center."

The concourse was deserted, and none of the lights were on, but the floor-to-ceiling windows let in a watery gray daylight. Tamia jogged over to the windows. Through the deluge, she saw the airport lit up in the distance.

Nic joined her. "No wonder the power went out."

Tamia checked her reception. "Still nothing. Is there a way to get back to the convention? Other than that hallway?"

"I'm sure the power will come on soon," Nic said. "Let's just wait a minute."

Now that they had escaped the maintenance corridor, Tamia was much less anxious. The empty concourse felt like the abandoned set of a science-fiction movie: wide, dimly lit, with glass walls and tall steel columns. Nic, in her costume, looked like she belonged here. Tamia wasn't so eager to get back to civilization. "Okay," she said, and sat down on the floor, leaning against the windows.

Nic lowered herself down too, stretching her legs out on the smooth tile floor. "So," Nic said.

"So what?"

"So, that was a little creepy."

"Yeah, I don't like the dark," Tamia admitted.

"I don't like crowds," Nic said.

They looked at each other, and when their eyes met, Tamia felt a surprising jolt of nerves. "I kept imagining that part in *The X-Files* where Tooms comes through the vent," Tamia said.

Nic's eyes widened. "No wonder you were so freaked."

"I wasn't *that* freaked."

"You were holding my hand."

Tamia tried to hide her embarrassment by laughing. "Okay fine, I was freaked."

Nic smiled. "Hey, isn't Agent Scully a physicist?"

"Yeah, why? She wrote her thesis on Einstein's twin paradox. Time travel, basically. She thought it could be possible, theoretically."

"Sulu's a physicist too. We have something in common."

"Something, huh?" Tamia said slyly.

"Something."

Tamia had to look away so that she didn't stare, but she kept thinking about the expression on Nic's face. Did she mean *something something* or *I was actually talking about physics*? Flustered, Tamia took out her flashlight, unscrewed the cap, and removed the batteries. "I don't know what happened to my flashlight in there."

"Do you ever read any *X-Files* fanfic?" Nic asked.

The question startled her. "A little. Why?"

"Just wondering who your ship is. Like, are you into Mulder, or do you think Scully is, you know, less straight than that."

Tamia nearly dropped the batteries. "Sounds like that's what you think," she said, and quickly slid the batteries into the flashlight.

"Maybe."

"Maybe?" Tamia tried to make the word sound meaningful.

"I've read some Scully-slash-Reyes stuff, but I never really thought that worked."

"Well, that's because Reyes was totally underdeveloped and not that great of a character." Tamia couldn't get the cap back on the flashlight.

"You didn't like her?"

"She was okay, but it was too late in the series. Those last few seasons just didn't work for me. I binge-watched the first six seasons on Netflix over a few months, but the last three took me a lot longer."

"I never watched the last couple seasons, but I did read the fic." Nic held out her hand. "Let me try."

Tamia gave her the flashlight. "And you like Scully-slash-Reyes."

"Well, I like Scully," Nic said. She lined up the cap at the end of the flashlight and screwed it back on. She pressed the power button, and the light came on. "Loose batteries."

Tamia took the flashlight back. "Thanks."

"She's so smart," Nic continued. "A physicist, a medical doctor, an FBI agent . . ."

"Definitely an overachiever," Tamia said.

"What about you? How much are you like Scully?"

Tamia tried to stop fidgeting with the flashlight. "I am obviously not an FBI agent."

"But your badge is so realistic."

"I'm good at Photoshop."

"See? Genius."

"Well, I am on the math team at school," Tamia joked.

"I knew it! Where do you go to school?"

"Westminster High. I'll be a senior in the fall. How about you?"

"I go to Fairview in Boulder. I'll be a senior too."

"So I have a question for you," Tamia said, risking a glance at Nic.

Nic sat up expectantly. "Ask me anything."

"Okay. What about you? Are you . . . like Sulu?"

"Well, I'm not the helmsman on a spaceship, although I wouldn't say no to that opportunity."

"Are you on the math team at your school too?"

"No. I'm sorry to say math is not my thing."

"What is your thing?"

"I want to do something creative, you know? Like work in Hollywood or something, behind the scenes. Produce stuff. I want to help make sure that someday movies do include people like gender-flipped Sulu and race-bent Scully."

"That's really cool." Tamia noticed that Nic had three small silver hoops piercing her right ear. In the quiet between them, the sound of rain pounding against the windows was a constant staccato.

"It's pretty serious out there," Nic said softly.

"Yeah," Tamia agreed. She should be worried, shouldn't she? She hadn't heard from Casey or Seb, and she had no idea how to get back to the other side of the convention center. But she was reluctant to get up off the floor.

Tamia took a deep breath. "So I have one more question for you," she said.

"Go for it."

Tamia cocked her head at Nic. "Is gender-flipped Sulu gay too?"

The double doors they had come through banged open. Tamia heard squelching footsteps. She scrambled to her feet, Nic beside her, both of them staring at the thing that stumbled through the doors.

• • •

"Hi!" the creature said, gasping. It was an amorphous grayish-greenish blob edged with stiff hairs like giant eyelashes, and as it wobbled across the empty concourse toward them, it left a slimy trail on the floor. "I think I saw you back there in that hallway."

The voice sounded like it belonged to a boy about their age, but the blotchy makeup covering his face made him unrecognizable. He looked like a cross between an amoeba and a hairy eyeball.

"Did you come from DenCon?" Nic asked.

"Yes!" the boy answered. "I'm lost! Do you know what's going on?"

Nic and Tamia traded glances. "The power went out and we're waiting for it to come back on," Tamia said.

"Probably same as you," Nic added. "What's your— who are—?"

"I'm Wesley Holmgren," the boy said brightly. "I mean, that's my name."

"Um, what's your costume?" Tamia asked.

"I'm a *Megavirus*."

"A what?" Nic said.

"A *Megavirus*," Wesley repeated. "It's a giant virus, with 1,120 genes. The genome is 1.259 million base pairs long. It's an ancient virus, found by French researchers near Chile."

"But viruses are microscopic, even *Megaviruses*," Tamia said dubiously. "You look like—you're like the Thing or something. The Blob. Weren't those movies from the fifties?"

"Nobody gets my costume," Wesley said glumly.

"Sorry, dude," Nic said. "Nobody gets mine either. Why do your shoes squish like that?"

"I drenched them in this goo—it was from a *Ghostbusters* costume kit. I wanted to represent cytoplasm. But it makes walking around kind of gross."

Tamia nodded politely. "Okay. Well, points for going all out."

"Do you know how to get back to DenCon?" Wesley asked.

"We think we're on the other side of the building," Nic said, "so we could go around the outside—"

"But it's raining," Wesley protested.

"No kidding," Tamia said.

"I don't think my costume's waterproof," Wesley said.

A buzzing sound jolted through the convention center, and the overhead lights blinked. With a hum, every light panel suddenly snapped on, bathing the concourse in a white glow.

"Power!" Wesley cried.

Off to their right, a digital display flickered to life. "I think that's a directory," Tamia said, and headed over to the monitor.

Nic and Wesley followed her to the bright touchscreen. Tamia pointed to the pulsing red dot that indicated YOU ARE HERE. "See, we must be in the west concourse," Tamia said. "We can take it to the end and then go down this walkway that connects to the east concourse and DenCon."

Nic's phone dinged and she pulled it out of her pocket. A text from her brother read: *Where are you? You okay?*

A series of chimes rang from Tamia's phone. "Finally!" she said, and began texting.

Nic responded to her brother and then said, "Should we head back?"

"Can I go with you?" Wesley asked. "I get lost really easily."

"Sure," Tamia said.

Nic suppressed a sigh. She would've been happy to be stuck alone with Tamia for a few more hours.

• • •

On the walk to the east concourse, Wesley regaled Tamia and Nic with the history of the *Megavirus,* also known as *Megavirus chilensis,* never letting either of them get a word in edgewise. As they approached the entrance to the convention, Tamia spotted a few cosplayers dressed like Wesley waiting by the entrance.

"That's *Mimivirus, Pithovirus,* and *Pandoravirus,*" Wesley explained excitedly, and pointed to the design on the front of his blob-like costume. "See, we've differentiated our markings to indicate our different genomes. I have to go meet them. Thanks for your help!"

"Sure thing," Tamia said.

"Yeah, no problem," Nic said.

Tamia stopped as Wesley ran over to his friends. She glanced at Nic, who seemed a little subdued. "Where are you headed?" Tamia asked.

"I'm meeting my brother over by registration," Nic said, gesturing to the right.

Tamia checked her phone. "My friends are waiting for me by the entrance to the Rocky Mountain Ballroom. That's where the *Queen of the East* preview was, right?" She pointed in the opposite direction.

"I think so. I guess this is it, then. It was nice to meet you."

Tamia smiled tentatively. "Yeah. If I had to be stuck in a power outage with a stranger, you're the one I'd pick."

Nic grinned. "Likewise. So . . ."

"So . . ." Tamia still couldn't read the expression on Nic's face. Was she waiting for Tamia to make the first move? Or was she worried about finding her brother? All the words Tamia could say were clogged up in her throat, blocked by uncertainty and nerves. Tamia's phone chimed again, like an alarm. *Time's up.* "I guess I better go," she said reluctantly.

"Yeah, okay." Nic started to turn away.

"Bye." Tamia waved at Nic, then felt like a dork. Who waved at a person two feet away from them?

"Bye," Nic said, raising her hand in response.

Disappointed, Tamia forced herself to turn away before she did something even more embarrassing.

• • •

Nic saw her brother standing near the registration booth with a phone held up to his ear. The concourse was full of confused con-goers and harassed-looking convention volunteers in hot-pink DenCon T-shirts. Nic slowed down as she approached her brother. Now that the power outage was over, she wasn't sure why she needed to find him anyway.

She thought about Tamia and that last question she hadn't had a chance to answer. *Is gender-flipped Sulu gay too?* Had she imagined the nervousness in Tamia's face? But also, hadn't the answer been obvious? That was the problem with being queer. You should never assume, but if you didn't assume, you had to ask. And asking directly was so hard to do.

"Nic!" her brother said. "You okay?"

"Yeah, I'm fine."

He ended his phone call and came over to her. "I have to

get back to the control room, but if you need to go home or anything—"

"No, I'll just—" She shook her head. She knew what she had to do. "I have to go."

Her brother looked surprised. "You have to go?"

"I'll text you later," Nic said, turning on her heel.

"Nic?"

"Later!"

She dodged a Harley Quinn, a Rogue, and two Iron Men, then began to jog as she reached the main concourse, following signs for the Rocky Mountain Ballroom. In the lobby outside, several DenCon volunteers were herding people into an orderly queue. Past the zombies—there were always zombies—and beyond the *Star Trek* contingent and the Gryffindor quidditch team, she finally saw the girl in a red Agent Scully wig. She was talking to two guys dressed in suits.

"Tamia!" Nic called.

Tamia looked around.

"Tamia!"

This time Tamia saw her. She broke away from the two guys, coming over to meet Nic. "What are you doing here?" Tamia asked.

Nic was a little out of breath, but she told herself it was because she had jogged from registration. "I'm looking for you," she said.

Tamia smiled. "You are?"

"Yeah. I need to ask you something."

The shorter guy Tamia had been standing with joined them. An FBI badge on his lapel identified him as Alex Krycek. "Mia, who's this?" he asked.

"This is Nic," Tamia said. "Nic, this is my friend Seb."

"Hey," Nic said.

"Hey back," Seb said. "Tamia said she met a girl, but I didn't realize she *met a girl*."

Tamia elbowed him. "Shut up."

"Ow!" Seb complained.

The other boy, who had a Mulder FBI badge pinned to his jacket, came over too. "Hey, guys, we have to get in line or we won't make it into the preview."

"This is the *girl* Tamia met during the blackout," Seb said.

Mulder looked sharply at Nic. "Oh, really?"

"Nic, this is Casey," Tamia said. She gave Casey a pointed look. "Casey, take Seb to the line and I'll meet you both there."

Casey grinned at Nic and grabbed Seb's arm. "Come on, leave 'em alone."

Seb waved at Nic. "See you later, I hope!" he said as Casey dragged him away.

"Those were my friends," Tamia said. "You know, Mulder and Krycek."

"I guessed," Nic said.

Tamia took a step closer to Nic. "So, you had something you wanted to ask me?" she prompted.

Nic felt her face heating up. "Um, yeah." She pulled out her phone before she could lose her nerve. "I was wondering if—if you want to meet up later. Can I get your number?"

Tamia broke into a wide smile. "Yeah, of course! Give me your phone."

Nic handed it over, their fingers brushing. While Tamia entered her number, Nic saw Seb and Casey lurking near the doorway to the ballroom. Seb gave her two thumbs-up.

Tamia returned the phone to Nic. "Text me so I'll have your number too."

"Bossy," Nic observed with a grin, but obeyed. "Just to be clear, you understand why I'm asking for your number, right?"

Tamia's phone chimed. She checked the message, then met Nic's gaze. She looked a little too long, just to make it extra clear. "Message received."

DON'T PASS ME BY

by Eric Gansworth

On the first day of Seventh, Hayley Sampson leaned against my homeroom's radiators. Her eyes said: "Do not blow my cover, Doobie, if you know what's good for you." The Rez school only took us to the end of Fifth, and then we were *merged* into the massive Junior High just beyond our border. There, among the nine hundred white kids and a handful of black kids, we each made decisions about how Indian we appeared, and we respected each other's choices.

Hayley snapped her eyes at the beadwork keychain on my backpack. Did she recognize it as one made by her aunt? *Margaret Sampson, June 1975* was written on the soft tanned leather backing. Even now, a year after Margaret had made it, the keychain held up. It was the gift I'd received at the Moving Up dinner held at our elementary school. Adult Beadwork Class members, mostly City Indian gramma types and younger Rez ladies, made them for all levels of Indian graduates: Elementary, High School, and College. The class members were relearning beadwork skills they'd lost, or learning stuff their own mothers had refused to teach them.

I didn't have any keys yet, so I just looped mine on my backpack's zipper tongue. My keychain was a Buck Head, and my last name was Buckman, so that was a cool matchup. The kids I *should* have left elementary school with, like Hayley, got a Turtle keychain at Moving Up. I loved mine, but the Buck Head reminded me that I'd failed Kindergarten. When you screw up Taking a Nap and Playing with Finger Paint, no one forgets. And if you did happen to forget, Carson Mastick had given me a helpful nickname: Hubie Doobie, the Flunked-Out Booby.

We each adapted to our new lives differently. Hayley and Carson wrapped themselves in white-kid hairstyles and clothes, but you knew they were Indians as soon as you saw them with us. Bill and Andy Crews, two cousins who I met in my Kindergarten do-overs, were dark like me. We had fewer options if we wanted to disguise ourselves. Older and bigger than every kid in my class, I stuck out. Even before my beaded keychain, I refused to try Passing for a kid from the Italian suburbs or Passing for a tanned farm boy. Strangers would know exactly where I was from. I have a big hawky Indian nose, thick lips, and long black hair tied back in a sneh-wheh, now past its second summer. When I didn't braid it, you could see it was uneven and split.

Hayley Sampson's dad was white, so people said she had

half-Indian blood, which I thought was bizarre. Did she bleed different colors depending on where she got cut? This half blood allowed her to almost cover up any visible trace of us. She was better at her disguise than Carson, and he moved easily between groups, like he wore Skin Camouflage. The only thing giving Hayley away were her Indian eyes. I don't mean that they had a melodramatic tear dangling out of them like a pull chain. They were just deep, deep brown, the color of a horse.

Last Spring, after her mom died, Hayley had racked up enough Days Absent to win herself a Repeat Year, and so we became classmates again. I thought I'd show her the ropes about being an official failure. But that first morning in homeroom, Hayley sported a new, wild look beyond the usual human colors. Her face shimmered like a powdery pearl, slashed with maroon lips and lavender eyelids. Heavy black liquid gave her crow's wings for eyelashes. Her purple-black hair was sprayed into an explosion on top of her head. It was like the white side of her had wrestled the Indian side down for the count, but they'd both come out a little rougher.

Since she was now with kids a year younger than her, and we were the only Indians in our section, she knew no one but me. I was used to flying solo, since my place as The Big Indian Kid made white kids nervous. By the middle of the day, she'd begun to sit next to me. We just sat together, silently pretending that we didn't live a road apart. I knew when it was safe to talk. Those Passing Indians, as soon as they got to the buses, suddenly they were Indian again, like Abraca-dabra. But if you tried to chat them up in school, prepare to be ignored. At the end of the day, I silently went to my locker and she went to hers.

"So you look kinda different these days," I said as we neared the safety bubble of Rez buses. "What's going on up in here?" I motioned around her head.

"Soon's I can, I'm signing up for BOCES," she said, as if she hadn't ignored me all day. "Gonna get my cosmetology license. Then, fast as we're out, I'll have the perfect job train-ing. Can't sign up until Ninth, so right now I'm practicing on myself and my old Barbie Glamour Head."

I nodded. My girl cousins had those heads too, perched on their bedroom dressers, slathered in makeup and sport-ing ratted spiky blond halos. The disembodied Barbie heads freaked me out. The Barbies reminded me of the scary Fly-ing Head in the stories our gramps told. He claimed those heads cruised around the Rez to catch kids awake past bed-time. After a while, I'd refused to go into my cousins' room. Sometimes one of those girls would chase me with the Barbie head, making haunted noises, if she felt especially evil and ambitious.

"You could use a sprucing up," Hayley added. "I could even those out." She touched the scroungy tip of my sneh-wheh, clucking at my split ends. In the two years I'd been growing my hair long, it had never been touched by a girl. A dumb guy might think this would change how we talked to each other, but I knew better. The next morning, as soon as we left the bus, she got Rez Amnesia again. I took what I could get.

"I hate this class," Hayley whispered, not looking at me as we walked into Health, the third week in.

"You ain't alone," I whispered back, staring at the weird scene on the floor. Everyone hated Health, where they forced you to talk in class about the things you were discovering on your own, in private. The first week, we blew through the safe units on Nutrition and Hygiene, like Flossing, the Dangers of Smoking and Gum Disease. The Stress and the Body Unit took up the second week. The textbook pictures weren't *real* Stomachs Under Stress, but instead drawings of pale pink organs, bunched like the paired socks your mom brought home from the laundry.

"Folks, I'd like you to meet Resusci-Annie," Mr. Corker said, hovering above this mysterious figure collapsed near his desk. He grinned, loving the small chaos he'd thrown us into, eyeing Hayley for any bad reaction. Were we supposed to go to our seats? Introduce ourselves? Were we supposed to gather around Annie, like he was trying to herd us?

We knew the splayed woman wasn't real. Her vinyl skin and scraggly straw-colored doll hair made her look like a special Rough Life Anti-Glamour Edition of the Giant Barbie Head Hayley had mentioned. This Annie at least had a body, but she seemed boneless or something. Her sneakered feet lay at weird angles, flat against the classroom floor.

"She's not breathing," Mr. Corker said, trying to sell us on the idea she was alive. The room filled with silence as we stared at the lifeless jogger. "Okay!" he said with a loud, awkward clap. "Resusci-Annie is a simulator, to help us learn to properly administer CPR." He paused and then elongated the next three words, "Cardio . . . Pulmonary . . . Resuscitation. Now, she is *not* a toy!" he added, as if we'd suddenly tried to play with her. "She's a lifesaver."

"That don't mean you can suck on her, Hubie," said Marco, one of the jerks in my class, his friends laughing. I wondered if Carson Mastick had told white kids that I'd failed Kindergarten, or if they'd just overheard him calling me Hubie Doobie the Flunked-Out Booby.

"Hey! Guys," Mr. Corker jumped in. "These are exactly the shenanigans I warned about. Health is no joke!" The laughers cupped hands around their grins, like TV chimps. I wondered if Mr. Corker himself had a Stomach Under Stress. This class used to do CPR toward the end of the year, but for us, it was going to be Week Three. Maybe the ghost of Hayley's mom and her heart attack haunted Mr. Corker. He'd been Hayley's teacher last year and here she was again. I didn't ask if she'd failed CPR or if they just hadn't gotten to it in time. He seemed super aware of Hayley when we walked in to find Annie, a waxy, blond, dead, loose-limbed jogger in a heap on our floor. Hayley looked down, matching Annie's blank stare.

"If you see someone in distress, you may be the only person around who knows what to do. Like Annie, you too could save lives. Think about it." He then performed the proper method, step by step. We had to ask Annie if she was all right, touch her neck to try to find a pulse. We were then supposed to lean over, place an ear to her mouth, and pretend she might answer and breathe when we knew she wasn't going to cooperate. Mr. Corker tilted Annie's head back, pinched her nose, took a deep breath, and then locked lips with her, repeating this sequence a few times.

"Looks like she's gonna hurl," said Tom, one of Marco's grinning chimps, when her body heaved, filled with Mr. Corker's forced breath.

"That what happens when you try to kiss a girl, Doobie?" Marco said to me, not bothering to cover his grin. Now that some guys had gotten growth spurts, they tested their manhood by poking The Big Indian Kid. They acted like they were Running with the Bulls, like we'd seen men do in our Social Studies Unit on Spain, except in this case, I was the bull.

"Marco!" Mr. Corker shouted, running an alcohol wipe along Annie's lips and onto her slightly exposed teeth. "Here, on the mouth! Tom, chest compressions."

"I don't know what that is," Tom said.

"You're gonna learn. Firsthand. Right now," Mr. Corker said, "since you can't seem to pay attention otherwise."

"What if I don't wanna?"

"Detention and an F for this Unit. Your choice." Tom and Marco grumbled, bumbling to the floor. Mr. Corker talked them through the CPR basics: checking and clearing Annie's airways, sealing her lips and pinching her nostrils closed, then breathing into her mouth.

"You need to find," he said, pausing, getting ready to speak a word he couldn't avoid, "her breast*bone*. To commence with proper chest compressions. Regularly check her neck artery for a pulse." Mr. Corker squeezed a bulb that sent air down a tube into Annie, giving her some artery action. He waited until Tom broke a sweat pushing up and down on Annie's chest, elbows locked, before he squeezed Annie's pulse bulb. Mr. Corker then alcohol-wiped her mouth and had Marco and Tom change places, working them hard again.

"All right, who's next?" Mr. Corker said as the jerks stood.

"Jacqui," Marco said, standing. "How about you let me find your breast*bone* to practice *proper chest compressions*? Get your pulse going?" Jacqui fake-slapped his chest, laughed, and stepped forward, volunteering.

"I'll do it," she said, kneeling easily, leaning her face into Annie's, taking her duty seriously. She looked amazing without even trying. She could be flirty, kind, and sensitive, take her grades seriously, *and* be dressed perfectly all at the same time. Other girls, Hayley included, could juggle maybe two of those things, but even there, it was touch and go. Jacqui floated on a cloud of her own Natural Amazingness.

"I'll do compressions," I said, kneeling next to her, still feeling like a Spanish bull, this close. If I made one wrong gesture, I might send tiny Jacqui flying across the room. Mr. Corker ignored the whispering chimps around us.

"Forget them," Jacqui said, touching my arm, her skin slightly warmer than mine. "We've got a life to save."

I tried taking her advice, but even compressing, I heard Tom say that I was just trying to get Jacqui's white-girl spit in my mouth the only way it would happen. I compressed so hard I felt like I might bust the spring in Resusci-Annie's chest. Marco said I wanted to see how wide Annie's mouth opened. They speculated that my locked elbows were clogged with embedded dirt, but my skin was just naturally darker there, and a few other places. When I was seven, I'd tried to scrub the color off my elbows so hard they blistered and bled. As I compressed Annie's chest in silence, one fist over the other, my ears burned deeper red.

"Oh, I forgot!" Mr. Corker said when we stopped. Resusci-Annie's lips wore the same frosted red that Jacqui's had. He dug into his desk for Kleenex and a jar of Noxzema. "Girls, and some of you guys, maybe, I don't know. Please wipe any makeup off *before* your turn. We don't want it staining Annie's skin. You want her to be *normal* colored for the people who come after you." Normal. Hayley and I locked eyes.

After final bell, safely within the private area near our Rez buses, Hayley came up to me. She'd reapplied her maroon lips, and outlined their edges to make them seem smaller, like Barbie lips. "How come you let those guys talk like that?" she asked, pretending she hadn't chosen to be deep under-cover, like cop show heroes trying to spy on criminals in their hideouts.

"I was the only Indian there," I said, and it was out before I could slam my big skut-yeah shut. "I just meant . . . *guy*! I was the only Indian *guy* there." But she'd already joined girls from her end of the Rez, safely in the bubble of our portable Rez on wheels.

From that day forward, she wouldn't even silently sit near me. I almost wanted to expose her disguise to the new girls she shared makeup tips with and the guys she flirted with, but I'd been followed in stores often enough to wish that I had more say in how others saw me. On the bus, no matter where I sat, she made sure to walk past, not even snapping her deep, horse-brown eyes in my direction. She wasn't going to waste energy making a face at me.

The week of Thanksgiving, Resusci-Annie long stored back in her suitcase, our classes were briefly segregated. We were supposed to cover a Very Special Unit they might as well have called the Line Drawings of Adulthood Unit. The girls from my class went with Ms. D'Amore, and the guys from her class joined us in Mr. Corker's room. If your parents didn't sign the permission slip, you were shipped off to the library to maybe conduct your own solo research on the Puberty and Reproduction Unit.

That week, I had a chance to talk to someone in class. Bill and Andy Crews, those two cousins I sometimes hung out with on the Rez, flopped down next to me. It wasn't hard for them to find seats. Between the TV chimps and the other kids afraid of The Big Indian, I had an armada of empty desks around me most days. Marco speculated to the other chimps that Mr. Corker might bring in *Playboys*. Carson Mastick's dad had more intense mags than the likes of *Playboy.* No way was Mr. Corker gonna pass those around to a bunch of Seventh-Grade guys.

Corker shut the door and positioned his overhead projector. Was our teacher really going to talk about boners or, even weirder, say the word *boner* aloud? When he slapped a transparency onto the projector and turned it on, I figured we were safely away from such talk.

Just like the other illustrations we'd been shown, the simple drawing didn't look like anyone's anatomy I'd ever seen. It resembled the clogged drains in the Liquid-Plumr commercials, except here, the downward-drooping pipe had a stubby, rounded end. The drawing had arrows pointing to specific parts. We were each extremely well versed in these particular parts on our own, but it was safe to guess that none of us had ever used the alien words printed at the end of each arrow tip. Like the Stomach Under Stress illustration, the main organ in this drawing was pale pink, the color of Shrimp Cocktail.

Corker handed out identical worksheets, but at the ends of the arrows, the words were missing. He told us to copy off the projection and memorize the new words. "No improvising with colorful language, now. We are young men, growing mature." I suspected that he hated this Unit the most, even worse than the recent Learning to Spot and Treat Lice Unit. "Part of that maturity is using proper names!"

We wrote the new words, passed the sheets forward, and waited. The next transparency-worksheet combo included the distribution of two slim boxes of colored pencils. I knew *for sure* it was the week Corker hated the most. This worksheet featured a line-drawn Naked Boy with generic features and similar stubby equipment. On the screen, Projected Naked Line Drawing Boy was also Shrimp Cocktail Pink.

Corker hit the screen with his rubber-tipped pointer and said this kid was our age, and that right around now, changes started happening. In his most soothing voice, he assured us these changes were *perfectly natural, perfectly normal.* Our voices would crack and lower, our Adam's apples would start sticking out, we might get zits, and we'd probably want to choose a deodorant to use *every day* (circling back to the Hygiene Unit). These changes had happened to me when I was ten. Even if I hadn't been a year older than everyone else in my class, this update still would have been old news to me.

"And now," he said, "as I mentioned, this may have already started happening with some of you guys—and I don't need to know; keep that info to yourselves, please—but *this* will happen." He dropped an overlay on top of Naked Pink Boy. On the screen, shapeless light brown blobs were now projected in Naked Pink Boy's pits and around his stubby pipe. Marco and Tom asked if we were gonna get tans in these places that didn't usually get tanned.

"Come on, guys," Corker said, sighing. "You know what this is. I mean, um, some of you are already trying *hard* to start peach-fuzz mustaches." He laughed a fake three-stutter burst, stroking his own bushy mustache without being aware he was.

As the two slim boxes came my way, I slid a colored pencil from each and passed the boxes to Bill and Andy. The boxes were not assortment packs. I looked at the two pencils and the words printed along their slim spines. *Flesh* and *Burnt Sienna*. The three of us, in our tiny desk Rez, looked at each other and shrugged. Andy started dutifully coloring in first. He frowned at his cousin, and Bill caved. They cupped their arms around their sheets, as if I would try to copy off of them. But I knew what they were really hiding, and I was definitely *not* going to take the same path they were on.

Even at the Rez school, they'd been Goody Two-Mocs types. They weren't super smart like Lewis Blake, who tried to Pass by getting all A+ Grades, but these two always worked to keep out of trouble. They stayed in Boy Scouts, even when we discovered we'd have to do a bunch of fake Indian crap to get badges. Everyone else dropped out, but Andy and Bill joined a troop just off the Rez, a couple of Living Mascots.

I picked up a colored pencil and started shading. Toward the end of class, Bill and Andy looked at mine, glanced sidelong at each other and then down at theirs. The five-minute bell rang. Mr. Corker took Naked Pink Boy and his brown fuzzies off the overhead projector and threw on another transparency that seemed pretty unlikely. On the screen, the image looked like a badly drawn buck head, with a couple of hard-boiled eggs hanging from the antlers.

"Tomorrow?" he said. "The female reproduction system." That drawing didn't look like anything I'd seen in the mags Carson's dad had. I was curious. "Please turn in your puberty drawings before you leave. Make sure your name's on them or you won't get credit. And, men? Please don't steal my colored pencils. I need them for next period."

"This your regular teacher?" Bill asked me. I nodded. "Does he really think we could screw up copying what he put up on the screen?"

"Asking the wrong person," Andy said. "Didn't you see?" He pointed with his lips at my worksheet. He turned to me and smiled. "You like Seventh as much as Kindergarten? Just do what they tell you, Doobie. Not everything's gotta be about proving you're Indian." They tossed their colored-in boys on Corker's desk and walked out. I waited until everyone else left and set my sheet on top of the stack. Corker said thanks but kept his head down, recording names. Finally, after he could no longer ignore my lingering bulk, he looked up.

"Something I can help you with?" he asked, irritation visible.

"I wanted to show you my work," I said.

"Just leave it on the stack. I'm sure it's—" He stopped when he saw what I'd done. I definitely had a Stomach Under Stress just then. Was mine pink like the one in our book, or darker brown like the various parts of my body? Whatever color it was, my stomach was bunched up and yelling at me to stop, but I'd gone this far. He probably knew I'd flunked at some point, but I didn't want him thinking *this* was a screwup.

"This color," I said, tapping the box of Flesh on his desk. "Its name doesn't cover everyone. Those other two guys from the Rez? They knew what you wanted to see. I'm not gonna do that." I had used the Burnt Sienna lightly to color all the Naked Boy skin, tracing neatly around all the lines, like they showed me both times in Kindergarten, to Stress Your Intention. I'd retrieved my regular No. 2 and colored the assigned pubes in black, and the pit hair, and I gave Naked Burnt Sienna Boy a long black sneh-wheh, like my own. I even left some of the ends a little broken, like mine were.

He glanced down at my paper. "I see. Hubert. But *you* know, the assignment wasn't a self-portrait."

"It *was,* if you're white," I said.

"My instructions were clear."

"I followed the instructions," I said. If only Hayley could hear how tough I was now! I'd screwed up with her, accidentally making her feel gone. I hadn't found the words to tell her what I meant. When I didn't speak up in class, it wasn't that I was afraid of Marco and Tom. I could pound their TV chimp asses if I wanted. But even not laying a hand on them, I'd be the one blamed for making trouble. They'd skip on through, like they always did. They didn't get that bold overnight, in the same way Billy and Andy didn't become Boy Scouts, Rule Followers, overnight either. I decided now to at least live up to the reputation I'd walked in with.

"Your pencils only allowed for one kind of boy," I said, tapping Andy's Naked Pink Boy with Burnt Sienna Pubes. He and Billy always obeyed. Their older siblings and cousins had the same talk that my older cousins had with me in Fifth Grade. They'd been told how the teachers were going to look at them. They looked as Indian as I did, but they decided to make themselves into Exhibit A. *Exhibit Apple,* the mean part of my brain whispered into my ear. *Red on the outside . . .* I wouldn't call them that to their faces. If they wanted to try proving they were Indian kids who didn't make trouble, that was their business.

"This kind," I said, tapping my drawing. "This kind becomes a man too. Pretty much the same way." That wasn't exactly true. I was beginning to understand how easy it was to be silent, to think of yourself as a vanished Indian. Everywhere you looked, you weren't there. I wondered to myself if the Resusci-Annie only came with blond hair and skin in one shade, the one the art pencil company simply called Flesh. But I didn't bother asking Corker.

I headed to the lunchroom, to catch Hayley before she sat with the white kids, not saving me a seat. Maybe she wouldn't pass me by today. When she grew up, she could decide who she was, which blood she claimed. Now she still lived with us. I might slide her my beadwork Buck Head keychain upside down, revealing her aunt's signature. I could imitate Mr. Corker's voice, asking her if she knew how to Label the Parts Using the Correct Anatomical Terminology. It was a Rez-style joke. Her friends wouldn't get it, or they'd act all shocked and offended.

With luck, I'd get her to laugh with me at stuff she used to find funny. Then maybe her makeup would smudge, just a bit. In my fantasy, I'd offer her my hand, its knuckles dark like my elbows and other parts. Together, we'd bust into Corker's classroom, and I'd snag the jar of Noxzema and the tiny Kleenex pack from his desk. Bill and Andy would have come prepared with both, but I was no Boy Scout. I could pass these things to her. Even beyond our Rez bus, maybe she'd wipe away the glittering pale layers she'd learned to build up, practicing on those giant Barbie heads. I'd glimpse the Indian girl I used to know. I'd look into those dark brown eyes, press my fingers lightly to her neck, where the makeup was thinner, and linger to feel a pulse.

BE COOL FOR ONCE

by Aminah Mae Safi

The thump of the bass and the riff of the guitar took Shirin to a higher plane, even if she was only listening to an opening act. At least, until Jeffrey Tanaka walked into the Fox Theater looking like a sex god after a particularly divine offering. He ran his hands through his dark hair, scanning the crowd. He pulled out a Chap Stick and swiped it across his lips. Like he'd decided to draw shining arrows to all of Shirin's favorite parts.

Helpless, Shirin could only stare. "What fresh hell is this?"

"That's unfortunate," said Francesca in total solidarity. Because Francesca understood, even if she was immune to Jeffrey's charms.

"Why is he at a Thousand Day Queens show? I know he's not supposed to be out on a school night. He told me his parents wouldn't let him. He's a *baseball* player. Why would he get them to make an exception for *this*?" Because this wasn't just an opener for any band. This was the Thousand Day Queens at the Fox, one of those preserved institutional theaters in downtown Oakland. Shirin had been bragging about her tickets all week. And the ability to be cool and relax while Jeffrey stood nearby was like knowing the speed of an electron and exactly where it was. *Impossible.*

"Aren't the Queens too girlie?" But Shirin knew the assumption was unfair as soon as she'd said it. The red pen she'd borrowed from him that morning bit naggingly into the back pocket of her jeans. She hadn't used a red pen in her entire life. She'd only started borrowing things in homeroom to talk to him and she'd only started talking to him to prove to herself that he wasn't as interesting as he looked. It hadn't worked. Once, she'd even borrowed a protractor from Jeffrey and she hadn't needed that, either. It was awful.

"If rock is girlie." Francesca shrugged. "Besides, they've just blown up."

True. That had cost them, too. Much more than the last time, back before the Queens were famous and before Shirin could go to a concert on a school night. She took off her glasses, cleaned them on her worn T-shirt, then put them back on, the way she did when she was in the middle of a difficult lab. The logic didn't add up. The data was, well, wrong. Incomplete. *Why was Jeffrey here?*

"What do you think of that roadie?" asked Francesca.

"Who?" Shirin's eyes were still glued on Jeffrey. He kept looking around the venue. A sickening thought bubbled through her—he was meeting someone here. Shirin was going to have to watch Jeffrey on a date while her favorite band played. She must have forgotten to think penitent thoughts about one of the Twelve Imams when she was at *masjid* last weekend, because Shirin was definitely being punished.

Francesca nudged Shirin with her elbow. "Friend, you are blind. The one in the beanie? She's back there. Stage right wing. And nobody helps her out. Perfect."

But Shirin was too busy following Jeffrey's movements to pay much attention. He waded through the other concertgoers, his eyes hopeful and sharp. He gently tapped a girl with dark hair on the shoulder, but his expression fell when she turned around.

And that's when he looked up and caught Shirin staring.

Shirin jolted, then froze, an electron trapped in the beam of a microscope. Her location known, she couldn't move. Jeffrey walked toward her.

"Deep breaths." Francesca patted Shirin on the back. "Channel Anne Bolcyn. Go after your man. Or throne. Whatever."

"Anne Boleyn lost her head." Shirin looked away from Jeffrey, hoping to forget he was headed her way. She had the heart of a scientist. She wanted to be a physicist, a professional observer, a watcher. Not an explorer or a gambler. "And her throne."

"Didn't say it wasn't without its risks." Francesca smirked. She was a pusher and an adventurer. The girl with the wild hair who could talk literally anyone into anything. The concert scene was her and Shirin's middle ground—sound waves, freed from the safety of the lab, pushing against a pit of people.

Of course Francesca had been the one to discover the Thousand Day Queens down one of her many rabbit holes in the Internet music forums. They had stage names and insane costumes and an ability to turn rock into art. The names had practically made Francesca convulse—they corresponded to *tragic* historical queens. Maria Antonio for Marie Antoinette, who had met her fate at the guillotine. Rana Jhan for *the* Rani of Jhansi, who died fighting for Indian independence from the British a hundred years before it actually happened. Ana Pembroke for Anne Boleyn, who was beheaded by her own husband. Women who had all reached for the stars and had crashed spectacularly back down to earth.

The thought of crashing, of risking exposure, made Shirin dizzy.

"I prefer to keep my head attached to my neck, if it's all the same." Shirin turned back to the crowd, but Jeffrey had disappeared. "And he looks like he's meeting someone. Like a date *someone.*"

Francesca laughed like Shirin had just told a good joke. "Try overreaching for once, friend."

"Overreach what for once?" Jeffrey popped out from behind the railing and stopped inches from Shirin. He shoved his hands casually into the pockets of his stupid jogger pants. He always wore jogger pants. Even before they were cool.

Shirin stared. His V-neck was a little bit more snug and his hair was just a little bit more tousled than normal. Why couldn't she have the decency to like a shy, nerdy boy who flew under the radar? Jeffrey looked like he should come with biohazard labels. *Warning: may cause obsessive three-year crushes.* "Francesca's a reckless friend who wants my downfall."

"True. At least then you'd have tried something new." Francesca nodded, then turned to Jeffrey. "I was talking about Anne Boleyn. Know her? Lost her head over a man."

Shirin could have strangled Francesca. Francesca offered a saintly smile in return.

"You mean Natalie Dormer in *The Tudors*? She was badass." Jeffrey pulled out his Chap Stick and used it.

Francesca snorted.

Shirin blinked. "She was queen of England for a thousand days."

"Damn," he said. "It's the band name. I missed that. That's what you were saying. I thought—" He shut his mouth.

"Well done." Francesca offered him a sympathetic pat. "Most dudes never get it. Unless they're obnoxious film bros."

"Bless Natalie Dormer, I guess." Shirin's sarcasm was aimed at Francesca, but its collateral damage landed on Jeffrey. Fine. Maybe he'd go and find whoever it was he had been looking for. Then Shirin could get back to being an observer rather than caught in the light of his electron microscope.

Francesca elbowed Shirin in the ribs. "I think what Shirin meant was, super of you to give a shit about her favorite band."

Jeffrey's mouth twisted. "I know it's your favorite band. I'm not *that* clueless."

Onstage, the opener reminded the crowd of their name and thanked everyone for listening. The scraping and lifting of instruments was all there was to distract Shirin from the thrashing *thump thump thump* in her chest. She was going to have to make it through this entire concert right next to him. She was never going to last.

• • •

Francesca narrowed her eyes. "Consider this your two-minute warning."

"For what?" Jeffrey asked.

"She's getting Denise a signed shirt," said Shirin. A safe topic. Francesca had promised one for her girlfriend, Denise, since she was home studying for her calculus test tomorrow. No way to feel foolish talking about Francesca's girlfriend.

Jeffrey scratched his hands through his hair. "The shirt she's wearing?"

"No." Francesca's eyes didn't stray. She was memorizing the rhythm of the roadies onstage. She wasn't planning on waiting after the show like an ordinary fan.

"What Francesca really wants," said Shirin, "is to bring back a really good story for Denise."

Jeffrey flashed his lopsided grin. "She's gonna get some serious purple heart emojis for that. I mean—it's cool. That's cool."

Shirin tried to smile, but the expression got stuck halfway

across her face. There were apparently no safe topics with Jeffrey. Shirin was reminded of the time he'd said he loved *The Fast and the Furious*. When Shirin had said she didn't get a movie about pointless car chases, Jeffrey had described the part where Paul Walker got all mushy over a tuna fish sandwich because he was so in love with Jordana Brewster. Like that was the best part. Like he was a hopeless romantic as well as an athlete and a sex god.

Biohazard: may cause heart to burst.

Shirin turned abruptly away from Jeffrey. The roadie who had been trailing behind all the others finally turned her back on the crowd. Without warning, Francesca hopped onstage, picked up a cord that was left behind, and walked into the wings. The stage was a full head above Francesca, security guards were posted on either side of it, and the theater was already packed with people. But nobody had seen her. And Francesca was not a girl who could get away with anything and everything. Her dark hair and dark skin usually ensured extra scrutiny. But Francesca acted as though she were invincible. As though she were Anne Boleyn reaching for the crown.

Jeffrey turned, gobsmacked, to face Shirin.

Shirin laughed so hard, she snorted. She clapped her hand over her mouth, a flush coloring her tan face. She lowered her hand and said, "She's an observable phenomenon."

"You don't have any secret hidden skills like that I need to know about, do you?" His hands went into the pockets of his joggers again.

Shirin blinked, almost like fluttering her eyelashes. "I can kiss my elbow."

"Prove it." A challenging glint entered Jeffrey's eyes.

Shirin couldn't look away. A voice in the back of her mind told her she ought to. But her eyes focused on him as she grasped her right elbow with her left hand, then lifted it to her lips, giving a quick peck. Easy peasy. Minus the fact that her fingertips were tingling and her head was buzzing and she was still staring into Jeffrey Tanaka's dark eyes.

Jeffrey mirrored her movements. But he came up short. He craned his neck and tugged his elbow to no avail. He couldn't reach. He looked up, defeated. "Damn."

Shirin laughed—*without* snorting this time. "I guess I just have to face it. You're not totally perfect."

Jeffrey raised one of his straight eyebrows.

Oh god. Shirin had admitted—out loud—that she'd thought Jeffrey was otherwise perfect. To his face. She'd violated the one sacred aspect of scientific observation. She'd changed the environment. She'd acted on her subject.

Warning: known life-ruiner present.

That's when Francesca jumped down from the stage. She held up a signed Thousand Day Queens shirt—the one they didn't sell anymore, with Marie Antoinette eating cake while Anne Boleyn played with a long saber and Rani of Jhansi sipped tea—and a backstage pass. Shirin looked pointedly away from Jeffrey. Jeffrey stared at Shirin. Francesca watched them both. Then the lights dimmed and the Queens walked onstage.

There was only one thing left for Shirin to do.

"Be right back." Shirin grabbed Francesca's pass and fled.

• • •

Onstage, Ana Pembroke, the drummer for the Queens, was ripping through her opening set. The sound beat through Shirin's chest. Nobody could drum like Ana. If there was any justice in this world, Ana was destined to be one of the greats. Unlike Shirin, who was next to a road case in a hallway backstage, hiding.

The Queens were the first concert Shirin had gone to without a grown-up around. They were the kinds of musicians to put on *a show*. A show she was now missing. All because she couldn't fully admit how she felt about Jeffrey. Maybe if she'd told him, he would have gone away and found whoever it was he'd been looking for from the start. And she would be watching the Queens right now, not sitting beside some unused band equipment that smelled like gasoline and slightly singed plastic.

"Please. I gotta check on my friend." It was a horribly familiar baritone, impossibly blocking out the sound of the drums.

Shirin looked around the side of the road case. Jeffrey was talking to the backstage bouncer. Shirin slunk lower, winding her arms around her legs.

"He's cool, I swear." This from Francesca. "And I think he's the only one who can help. What if he closes his eyes? You're not really backstage if you gotta close your eyes."

"Backstage is backstage," said the backstage bouncer.

"Aw, honey," said a woman's voice. "Cut the poor kid some slack."

There was a long silence. Shirin didn't dare breathe.

"Fine," said the bouncer. "But you start any trouble and you're out of here, you got it?"

"Understood." Jeffrey's shoes squeaked as he walked.

Shirin peered over the back of the case. Jeffrey was about to walk right past, when his foot caught on the edge and he tripped. Jeffrey caught his balance, but the case toppled into Shirin's knee, causing her to yelp.

There was absolutely no justice in this world.

Jeffrey stopped, looked down. "Shirin, is that you? Are you okay?"

No. She was not okay. "Jeffrey. What are you doing here?"

Behind him stood Francesca, her eyebrows raised so high they met her hairline. The bouncer, with his STAFF tee and his surly expression, just stared. Shirin pushed the road case upright.

"You know you're the only one who calls me Jeffrey? Everyone else says Jeff."

As if Shirin needed another reminder that she was different from everyone. "No kidding."

They had drawn a small crowd. Sure, roadies backstage were pretending like they were going about their business. But they lingered as they wrapped up cords. They checked their mics in slow motion. They shuffled precariously close to the case Shirin hid behind.

Wonderful.

Shirin stood. "How did you get back here? And what are you doing *here,* at this concert?"

"I hoped I'd find you." Jeffrey stared, his eyes wide and honest.

I hoped I'd find you. That was worse than anything. The possibility of him only made Shirin wish she could be an adventurer like Francesca. Someone who enjoyed making history, didn't mind being observed. Shirin took a step back. She didn't know how to watch and be brave at the same time. She didn't know how to stay independent and be attached to Jeffrey.

Shirin could have cried. She was going to have to tell him how she felt. It was the only way he'd understand. She couldn't easily live her life under a microscope, not the way he did. She couldn't take that risk.

She took a deep breath. There was no going back from this. "Jeffrey. I've been in love with you since forever."

Nobody was even pretending to wrap cords anymore. And Francesca, who was shocked by nothing, gasped.

Shirin's voice shook, but she barged on. She had to make him understand. She was retreating. "I thought if I got to know you in homeroom, I would like you less. I thought we would be too different. But turns out, I like hearing how different you are from me. I've made it so much worse. You're not for me. You're not for girls like me. I'd rather see than be seen."

Jeffrey looked ready to take a step forward, but then he didn't. He nearly reached out for Shirin. But the woman with the boots tutted. Shirin looked over to her—she wore cherry-red lips and her raven hair in big, natural curls under a beanie. She reminded Shirin of a particle collider—power and precision.

"Uh-uh, kiddo," said the woman, her voice deep and rich. "You heard the man. No scenes, no trouble. I don't care how handsome you are."

Jeffrey groaned but stayed, miraculously, in place.

Shirin stepped closer to him, so he knew where she stood. "I'm going to leave and you're not going to follow me, could you do that?"

Shirin watched as Jeffrey opened his mouth again. His beautiful, stupid mouth. He closed it, clamping his lips shut. Jeffrey nodded.

"Thanks." Shirin didn't turn around as she left, because she didn't think she could bear it.

. . .

Above Shirin and Francesca, the Thousand Day Queens played like there was no tomorrow. There was only now, only this. It was the balm that Shirin needed to soothe her desperate heart. The lead singer and guitarist, Maria Antonio, had a voice of smokeless fire that melted into the sound of her wailing guitar. Everything about bassist Rana Jhan was steady and dependable. Rana was all hard work, absolutely no flash. Except for her pink hair that matched her instrument. Shirin had to admit, that was *some* flash. But it was the kind you expect from a band.

Francesca was in the same state of amped-up bliss—arms

in the air, eyes half-shut, feet thumping against the theater floor. They moved as a mass. A shifting, undulating beat across bodies. A particle and a wave. Shirin was sweating by now—Francesca's face glistened and her shirt was darkened in spots—but Shirin didn't feel the heat anymore. She shut out everything that wasn't rhythm and sound. The Queens played on and Jeffrey Tanaka ought to have been washed clean from Shirin's mind.

But under the beat of the drum Shirin could feel the thump of her heart. And in the twang of the bass, her memory reminded her of the squeak of Jeffrey's shoes. Shirin closed her eyes. If she couldn't conquer this now, she would at least pretend to. She did her best to give in to the music.

A full set and two encores later, Shirin could feel the scratches down her throat from screaming. She could sense the cramps in her calves that she would have tomorrow from jumping up and down tonight. She relished the feeling of her body being spent, of having left all of herself in the pit. Then she thought of Jeffrey trying to kiss his elbow and her euphoria did an unfortunate loop through her stomach.

"That was magic. Even knowing we were upcharged by a million percent." Francesca tugged at Shirin's arm, pulling her along toward the doors.

But Shirin caught sight of the exit and snatched her arm from Francesca's grip. Ahead, Jeffrey leaned on the wall beside the only open exit. There was no avoiding him.

"Oh no. I've really *got* to figure out which of the Twelve Imams I pissed off so I can beg forgiveness."

Francesca looked between them. "Hell no. I am not hanging around for this. Meet me outside when you're done."

"Outside?" croaked Shirin.

Francesca gave Shirin a quick kiss on the forehead. "I told the girls we'd get shawarma on Grand after the show. Obviously you're coming with. The ridiculous athlete is also welcome."

"The girls, as in the Thousand Day Queens?" Shirin shook her head. "Who *are* you?"

Francesca shrugged and began walking away. "Your best friend."

"And I'm not asking him," shouted Shirin, but Francesca was already outside. Francesca and her tough love. She would pay for this. Someday soon.

Shirin approached Jeffrey and the inevitable. But she didn't know what to say. She'd used up all her words backstage. She stopped and stared, feet from him, thinking about elbows, and Chap Stick, and tuna fish sandwiches.

Jeffrey ran his hands through his hair. "You're infuriating."

"Me?" breathed Shirin. "How?"

"You convinced your parents to let you go to concerts when you were fourteen with research and a PowerPoint. Immigrant parents. I mean, I only have immigrant grandparents. You don't give a damn what anyone thinks of you. Like, you always say what's on your mind. And, one day out of nowhere, you asked me for a pencil. Then a ruler. You don't just talk to anyone. So I kept ordering random school supplies in case you needed an orange highlighter or a protractor or a drafting ruler. I wanted to make sure I had it, if you asked." Jeffrey stubbed his toe on the floor. "And you even like me. So. Why—why do I have to stay away? Why are you staring at me like I'm contagious or something?"

Shirin took off her glasses and cleaned them on her shirt. She put them back on. "Because you're impossible. You have to be."

Jeffrey stared. "Why?"

Because she didn't know how to be an observer and an explorer. Because she didn't know how to be brave and be herself. "I didn't want to want you."

He laughed. It was hollow. "That bad, huh?"

"Worse," she said. And it was true.

Jeffrey turned to leave. He took one step. Then another. He wasn't going to turn back around, like at the end of a stupid car-chase movie. He'd probably get over this eventually. Shirin might, too. But maybe, if she was being honest with herself, she didn't want to. Maybe she hadn't started talking to him to prove he was uninteresting. Maybe she'd been taking a risk. Maybe all hypotheses were risk and all experiments were bets. Because maybe, just maybe, astronauts weren't only space explorers—they were scientists, too.

"I have my own protractor," she called out.

He turned around, his face blank. "Then why—?"

"Bullshit, asshole. No one likes the tuna here," she said. She hoped she was quoting the right line. She wasn't sure if that also made her the Paul Walker of this potential relationship, though. Better than being Anne Boleyn, to be honest.

"You watched it." He stepped closer. "You watched a pointless movie about car chases."

"You came to see a band you'd never heard." She shortened the distance between them to centimeters, then millimeters.

Shirin was close enough to run her fingers through his hair. She didn't, though, not at first. She just stood there, with next to nothing and all of infinity between them. Then she reached up—for his hair, for the stars—and for once didn't think about the consequences. It was as prickly as she'd imagined. He leaned into her hand, as though the touch were wanted. Then Shirin held his face and pulled his lips to hers. For a moment, he stood so still that Shirin thought she'd made a terrible mistake. And then he was kissing her back. Jeffrey Tanaka—with the sex god hair and the never-ending school supplies—was kissing her back. He tasted like spearmint. The hazy scent of the venue lingered on his skin.

When they broke apart, they were both short of breath. Jeffrey smiled from ear to ear. Shirin returned the grin. She took his hand and pulled him outside, knowing she'd have another fight with her parents ahead of her. This would *definitely* make for an interesting PowerPoint.

"Come on," she said. "We've got a date with a band."

They were still holding hands when Francesca waved them over. She was whispering something to Rana, like they'd already become the best of friends. Shirin laughed. If Francesca couldn't stumble on adventure, she made it happen through sheer will. Shirin was pulling Jeffrey along, nearly to Francesca and the band, when a shout stopped them both in their tracks.

"Jeffrey Tanaka, you get your butt in this car right now."
Shirin and Jeffrey jumped, releasing hands. At the curb,
Jeffrey's mom was leaning out the driver's side window of a
champagne SUV. Shirin sighed.

If only her life could be cool, for once.

TAGS

by Walter Dean Myers

Players

"BIG EDDIE" JONES, 17 . . . . "SMOKE"

WILLIE JIMENEZ, 16 . . . . "2-SOON/121"

D'MARIO THOMPSON, 16 . . . . "DATRUF"

FRANK WATKINS, 17 . . . . "J-BOY"

*We are in the present time. The play opens on a dingy urban
hallway in some dingy urban city. There is a door at stage right.
To the left of the hallway, next to stairs that go up at a steep angle,
we see* BIG EDDIE, *a young African American male, writing his
tag on the wall. From somewhere a radio is playing, and we hear
an* ANNOUNCER *talking about the wonders of the "oldies."*

*The light flickers occasionally, giving the set an eerie feeling.
The radio gets randomly louder, then softer.* BIG EDDIE *works
hard at his tag, which is the letters spelling out "smoke" sitting*

on a bed of flames. Throughout the play, the teenagers work on their tags.

The door at stage right opens and WILLIE *appears. He looks around and is momentarily startled by* BIG EDDIE.

WILLIE

Yo, what's happening?

BIG EDDIE

Same old, same old. Ain't nobody much in this building.

WILLIE

Do it count?

BIG EDDIE

Yeah, we still tagging, man. We still tagging. You got more paint?

WILLIE

Enough. *(He starts putting his tag on the wall. His tag reads* 2-SOON/121.*)*

BIG EDDIE

Where did you say you lived? East side, right? Over near Marcus Garvey Park?

WILLIE

Yeah. This your first wall tonight?

BIG EDDIE

First wall. Hey, man, you scared?

WILLIE

No, I ain't scared. You know some dudes just give up, but I ain't stopping, man. I got to hold on. How about you?

BIG EDDIE

When that old dude told me you could still be in the world as long as people kept you in their minds, I knew what I had to do. They see these tags and they remember. I felt stronger when they had the candles and a picture of me in the park. But the sanitation department took all that stuff away.

WILLIE

That's where you went down?

BIG EDDIE

Yeah. I thought I had a get over, man. Some Puerto Ricans said they wanted to cop some heavy weed. Five pounds of Jamaican. I told this dude to meet me in the park and he said okay. When he showed with the money, I tried to take him off, and he flashed a badge on me.

WILLIE

A cop.

BIG EDDIE

Yeah. I had my piece out and was about to hit the dude, when his partner shot me.

WILLIE

Damn!

BIG EDDIE

I knew I was gone. I could feel my heart, like, fluttering. Then there was people all around. I could make some of them out. Then it was over.

WILLIE

It's a funny feeling when you know you . . . you know.

BIG EDDIE

Man, I wasn't accepting it—you know, like I was looking the other way until they started putting flowers and some of my personal stuff around. They put out shit for you, too?

WILLIE

Yeah. Somebody made a sign—REST IN PEACE. That's a trip, right?

BIG EDDIE

How you like my tag?

WILLIE

(goes over and inspects BIG EDDIE'*s tag)* It's okay, but you should get some color in it. You got a fire, but it don't have any colors. If it's just black and white, people think about cleaning it off faster.

BIG EDDIE

Yeah, yeah. What you mean, "that's a trip"?

WILLIE

(returning to his own section of the wall) What?

BIG EDDIE

You said they put out REST IN PEACE and then you said it was a trip. Why you say that?

WILLIE

We resting? We ain't resting. Them old dudes said that as long as people remember us, we can still deal. We got our tags on the wall and people can see we were real, and they're thinking about us. But we ain't resting because we got to stay ahead of people cleaning the walls.

BIG EDDIE

I'm running from wall to wall to get my tag up. I'm getting tired. That's what happens to the old dudes. They get tired. They give up.

WILLIE

I ain't giving up. I'll tag for fucking ever.

The door opens again and D'MARIO *enters. He steps inside, then stops and looks at the others without speaking. For a moment they are frozen in place.*

BIG EDDIE

He's dead. He can see us, so he's dead. Yo, this hallway ain't big enough for everybody! Go someplace else.

D'MARIO

No place is big enough for everybody.

BIG EDDIE

So why don't you find another wall?

D'MARIO

You hear they cleaned up Malcolm X Boulevard from 120th Street all the way up to 135th?

WILLIE

Some guy is doing a documentary on Harlem. That same dude who did a thing on baseball. After they finish the shooting, they'll stop cleaning.

BIG EDDIE

They got a chemical now—you just spray it on and wait for a minute and then wipe it right off.

WILLIE

If he got an interesting tag, maybe they'll leave it up. People like art. What's your tag?

D'MARIO

DATRUF.

WILLIE

Yeah, yeah, I seen your tag. It's nice, man.

The door opens again and FRANK "J-BOY" *enters. The recognition scene is repeated and they all see that they are deceased.*

WILLIE

This place is getting to be like some kind of ghetto. How many tags going to go on one wall?

J-BOY

I ain't leaving. You got no power over me, sucker.

D'MARIO

Fool's dead and still talking smack! And tagging with a spray can. That's old. You can't tag with no spray can.

J-BOY

I can. I'm the best.

WILLIE

Yeah, everybody's the best, but we all went down.

D'MARIO

How you go down?

WILLIE

On a humble! I went into this bodega to get some cigarettes, and the owner—this old fucking dude—is eyeing
me like I'm fixing to steal something. So just out of spite,
I put my gun in his face. He panicked and started saying something in Spanish and English about "just take the
money." But he grabs hold of my nine and he's afraid to
let it go.

D'MARIO

'Fraid you going to do him!

WILLIE

Yeah, and all I want to do is get some cigarettes, let the fool
know I *could* have robbed him, and walk out the damned
door! But now I'm struggling with this old man and he's
holding on to my gun and crying and begging and carrying on. I ain't letting the gun go and he ain't letting the
gun go. Then two sisters come in and see what's going
on and duck right back out. I think they might be calling
the cops or something, so I let go of the gun with one
hand to punch the old man, and it goes off and hits me in
the neck.

D'MARIO

You killed yourself!

WILLIE

No! The old man had his finger on the trigger! The shot broke something in my neck and I didn't feel nothing. I knew I was on the ground and . . .

(WILLIE *is breathing heavily as he remembers the moment.*)

I thought I was just hurt bad. When the ambulance guys got there and looked me over, right away they started making nice-nice to the dude who shot me, trying to make *him* feel better. Then they put me in a bag and started . . . (WILLIE *can't continue.*)

WILLIE

(to D'MARIO*)* How you go?

D'MARIO

Why we got to go through all this? Ain't no use to it.

WILLIE

What else you got to do? You giving a lecture down at the college? You talking at the UN? Maybe you going to be on television!

D'MARIO

I was with my cousin Pedro and his little sister on his stoop. We were just chilling. We were talking about this and that, you know, light stuff. Then a car pulls up. Two guys get out of the car, and one of them asks where Hamilton Heights is. Pedro stands up and is going to give the guy directions, when I see he's flashing signs. One guy pulls down his cap and he's covering his face, so I knew some shit was about to go down! Then *blam! Blam! Blam!* Pedro ducks into the building, pulling his sister, and I'm right behind him. A bullet hits the wall next to my head, but I'm halfway up the first flight of stairs, so I think I'm cool. We get up the stairs, and I know they ain't about to follow us into the building, so I'm breathing light. I think I got a stitch in my side from running so hard, but when I look down, I see I'm bleeding. All kinds of crazy thoughts are going through my mind. You know what I'm thinking? I've been shot, but I'm still walking, dig? I'm like Fifty Cent and Tupac and all those guys who been through the battles. I wasn't even going to say nothing to Pedro until later. Some people are out in the hall 'cause they heard us running up the stairs, and a little boy points at me and tells his mama I've been shot. Then I look down again and my whole side is covered with blood. I sit on the stairs and they call 911 and the cops come and an ambulance. After that, all I remember is lying on a table and some doctor telling me to count backward from ten to one. I come to and I'm all by myself and there are guys like y'all standing around sucking on hurt and looking miserable.

WILLIE

They shot you for nothing?

D'MARIO

I tried to figure it out. About a week before, me and Pedro was in this hall right here.

BIG EDDIE

Where we are now?

D'MARIO

This white boy said he had some Mexican blow to sell. I thought he might have been a cop, but he sounded like he was from the South or something, so we thought he might have been legit. We was looking at the blow when another dude came rushing through the door. I thought he was a cop and I can't do no more bids, so I lit the mother up. It turned out that the white boy was legit, and the guy I shot lived in this building. So I figured the drive-by was some revenge.

J-BOY

In this building?

D'MARIO

Yeah. Yeah. So I read the whole set wrong, and then I got killed behind it!

J-BOY

(staggers against the wall) Oh, man! Oh, man. This is so fucked up!

BIG EDDIE

Hey, man, shit happens, bro! This is what our lives were always like. We out looking to make a name for ourselves and staying in the sunlight. We doing the same thing now.

J-BOY

No, man, it ain't like that.

BIG EDDIE

He's right. Being alive ain't tagging. Being alive is walking the damned streets, and making love, and listening to some music. This is just hanging on to what you know is already gone. This ain't nothing like no life.

WILLIE

Yeah, but this nigger getting all sick over it and shit don't help, either. We just got caught up in it, that's all.

J-BOY

(reaches for D'MARIO but goes through him) You killed me, motherfucker! You killed me! You killed me!

D'MARIO

What you talking about? What you talking about?

J-BOY

I came through the door that night! I had to pee and was rushing to get upstairs, when I seen a white boy with his back to me. He moved aside and all I saw was the flash from the damned gun! It was you! You killed me!

D'MARIO

Whoa, man, your boys got me!

J-BOY

I didn't have no boys. I don't know who got your ass! Maybe some baby Gs making their bones—I don't know! I know you killed my ass. You killed me!

WILLIE

This hallway is spooked, man. I'm going to go tag someplace else.

BIG EDDIE

Yeah, I gotta get some air. Gotta get some air.

D'MARIO

Man, I didn't know what was going on. It was an accident!

J-BOY

(tries to grab D'MARIO *again but again reaches through him)* I hate you! You shit-bitch motherfucker!

(He reaches for D'MARIO *again, but then stops as he real-izes it's hopeless. He repeats himself, but in a much subdued voice.)*

You shit-bitch motherfucker!

BIG EDDIE

I'm outta here! *(He starts slowly away.)*

WILLIE

(also leaving) Word.

D'MARIO

You can't do nothing to me now. I can't do nothing to you. It's too late. The shit is over. We can't turn it back.

BIG EDDIE, WILLIE, *and* D'MARIO *leave.*

J-BOY *sits and buries his head in his hands. We hear the sound of sobbing through the theater's loudspeakers.* J-BOY's *shoulders begin to shake as the sobbing fills the entire theater. It continues as* J-BOY *gets up and goes to the wall. Carefully he begins removing the tags of* BIG EDDIE, WILLIE, *and* D'MARIO. *He touches his own tag with his fingertips and then slowly wipes it away.*

WHY I LEARNED TO COOK

By Sara Farizan

Making out with Hannah Michaud was the most glorious thing to have ever happened in the history of the world. We had been officially dating for four months. Everything was exciting and new. We didn't wear matching T-shirts or kiss in public, but it was not lost on the student body that we were an item when she showed up to my girls' varsity volleyball games and I showed up to her photography exhibit. We were cuddly cute. It was perhaps a little nauseating, but I loved it.

Finding places to be amorous had been a little challenging. We often resorted to the backseat of my brother's red Ford Mustang that he couldn't take with him to college in NYC. My parents had met Hannah and liked her but always made sure my bedroom door was open when she visited. To be fair, they had done the same thing when my brother would bring over his now ex-girlfriend, so it was a step toward equality, I guess.

When we came up for air in the back of the car, Hannah grinned at me.

"And at one time you were so shy," she said. She laughed as I blushed furiously. To our peers we may have come across as an odd pair. Everything Hannah did was with exuberance and joy. Not in a corny, superficial way. She oozed free spirit and didn't seem to have any pre-occupations with high school cliques or SAT prep. She did whatever she wanted and I was a little envious of that.

I was . . . well, me. Tall—about five ten—athletic, I al-most always wore a high ponytail. I liked structure. I liked to have a plan. I liked to have my assignments done before they were due and didn't understand why Hannah would leave everything for the last minute. I worried about everything all the time. Hannah didn't seem to get anxious about anything.

"Well, I have my moments of courage," I said as I gently wrapped a strand of her brown curly hair around my finger.

"Sometimes," Hannah said kindly. There was, however, a hint of passive-aggressiveness. I knew what she was getting at.

My Friday nights were usually taken up by dinners at my grandmother's home. I had come out as bi to my parents a year ago, but I hadn't told my grandma yet. There didn't seem to be any point, since up until now I didn't have much of a love life. That is, until there was Hannah. I hadn't yet introduced her to my grandmother, nor had I planned on doing so anytime soon.

"You up to anything tomorrow?" I asked.

"Depends. I am very popular," she said, straight-faced. She was making fun of my describing her as such at one time. She would never let me forget it. "I am free for sure tonight, though."

"You really want to spend time with my grandma and her friend on a Friday night?"

"I would. I just want to know why you don't want me to. Are you worried she'll be upset or that she won't like me?"

I wasn't sure how my grandma would react. We were close, but the conversations between us were always about the past or the future. She didn't have any regard for the present, I guess.

"It'd be weird even if you were a guy. I mean, I don't know. I don't think she thinks of me doing stuff in a romantic capacity or whatever," I said, shifting my body away from her a little.

"It wouldn't have to be a huge coming-out thing, Yasi. You could just introduce me as your friend."

"She'd guess you were more than that," I said. My face would give me away. It was one of the things Hannah said she liked about me, my transparent feelings, particularly when she was around. It was how she had known I liked her. When Hannah walked by me or tried to make small talk, my face would flush and I'd stammer. She was the one to ask me out. I wouldn't have asked her because I never would have dreamed she could actually like me too. I was a bit of a chickenshit.

"I suppose she would. Anyone would, really," she said. I stuck my tongue out at her. When she smiled at me, my insides felt like I was made up of the remnants of the blown-up and torched Stay Puft Marshmallow Man. The Stay Puft residue sliming up my gut wouldn't let me fully relax around her. It was kind of scary liking someone this much. "Mostly I just want to eat homemade Persian food. Her importance to you is secondary," Hannah said with a grin.

"I'll keep that in mind," I said. Everything that Hannah had said that afternoon ended up being on my mind at Grandma's.

• • •

The inside of my grandma's home sometimes felt like a shrine to her family, as photos of her siblings, late husband, kids, and grandkids overflowed her small living room. There was almost no room on any of the end tables or coffee table, because all the space was taken up by framed photographs. Most of the frames had pictures of me throughout the years. It was a little unnerving to have my whole life unfold in front of me while I drank tea.

There were only two photographs of my grandfather. One was a black-and-white from their wedding day, he and Grandma smiling as they sat at a dinner table. Another was just of him, solo, in a suit, looking very serious. I had never met my grandfather. He passed away in Iran before Grandma immigrated here. My dad, a U.S. citizen, was concerned

that his mom would be alone and got a green card on my
grandma's behalf. It had apparently been a difficult and long
process, but she came over here when my big brother was
four and I wasn't born yet. Seventeen years later, I sometimes
worried she didn't always feel at home.

"Befarmaeed shaam!" Grandma said to Mrs. Khodadian,
her best friend who lived in the apartment above, signaling
that we were welcome to the dinner table. She had prepared
far too much food, expecting more than just the two of us.
My aunt and her family were at a wedding, my other uncle
and his wife were away on vacation, and my parents were too
tired, which I thought was a lousy excuse. It seemed like, as
the years went by, Grandma's dinner nights had become an
afterthought and something that was okay to skip.

Grandma had prepared a billowing platter of long-grain
basmati rice with saffron on top, two stews, salad Shirazi, and
bell peppers stuffed with meat, lentils, and rice. Her hand trem-
bled a little as she poured us doogh from a pitcher. I always
told Grandma that I thought doogh, a carbonated yogurt drink
with mint, was gross, but she still handed me a glass every time
and told me that if I tried it again I would like it. It never took.

"How is school, Yasaman?" Khanoum Khodadian asked
me in heavily accented English.

"Oh, um, it's good," I said in English. I could understand
and speak Farsi, but I was always embarrassed by my accent
when I spoke. It would also take me a while to adjust and
I'd occasionally use Farsglish, when I would jumble the two
languages together. Like, I'd forget a word in Farsi and use
the English word instead.

"She is such a good student! Did you know she has straight As?" Grandma bragged to Khanoum Khodadian in Farsi. Grandma didn't feel the need to speak English in her home with just Khanoum Khodadian and me. My grandma understood English and could communicate pleasantries, but if a conversation ever went a little too fast or there were words she missed, she would become very quiet.

Khanoum Khodadian did know I got straight As, because Grandma brought it up every time they saw one another.

"Did you watch your show?" I asked the ladies in English. I was happy to take some of the attention away from me.

"Oh yes! They voted off my favorite! I don't know why they voted her off," Grandma responded.

Grandma loved *Dancing with the Stars*. Actually, she had an affinity for all the variety talent shows, whether they involved singing, dancing, magic, pets doing tricks, but *Dancing with the Stars* was her absolute favorite. What I found most amusing about it was that she didn't know who any of the "stars" were. She'd describe the contestants as "the one with the sick mother" or "the one who used to play some sport but is now balding."

"Did you vote for the singer to stay?" Khanoum Khodadian asked her.

"It wouldn't have made a difference if I had. Besides, I don't think it's very fair when they have Olympic athletes or football players compete against older actors and singers. Of course the athletes will have an advantage," Grandma said.

My phone buzzed. Both ladies looked at me. My phone

almost never buzzed. I ignored it. I didn't want to be rude at the dinner table.

"Answer it! Maybe it's your parents deciding to join us," Grandma said, hopeful in a way that made my heart break for her.

It wasn't my parents. It was a text from Hannah.

I'm sorry if I pushed you about grandma today. I just know she means a lot to you. And you mean a lot to me. So it's like the transitive property in math.

"Who is that?" Khanoum Khodadian teased in English. My face had probably given me away again.

"Oh, um, it's a friend from school."

"I know my friends don't make me turn the color of a pomegranate," Grandma said in a playful tone.

I put my phone down and covered my mouth with my palm so they couldn't see me smile. I wanted my grandma to know who made me blush, but didn't think it was the appropriate time to break the news. But then, when would be an appropriate time?

"Grandma . . . do you think you could teach me how to cook?" I asked. Both women looked shocked. It was as if I had told them I was going to be a contestant on *Dancing with the Stars*.

"Oh, I never thought this day would come." Grandma held her hands to her chest. She had always been upset by the fact that my idea of cooking was heating up burritos in the microwave.

"You have made your grandma so happy," Khanoum

Khodadian said as she fanned Grandma, who was pretending to pass out.

I texted Hannah back.

How committed are you to vegetarianism?

Meat was kind of a huge staple in Persian cuisine. Figured I should learn menu items Hannah could eat.

Tell your grandma not to worry. I'm not going to convert you. ;)

I laughed at that. My grandma and Khanoum Khodadian took notice and smiled at one another but didn't say anything.

• • •

I usually took Grandma shopping on Sundays. Today we were also buying ingredients for the dishes Grandma was teaching me to make.

I pushed our full supermarket cart in the checkout line behind Grandma. The store was always crowded, no matter the time of day or night. I put Grandma's everyday stuff onto the conveyor belt.

"Hello. How are you?" Grandma said in her heavy accent to the man behind the register.

"Hi there," he said politely as he unenthusiastically scanned our items. The woman behind me with a toddler in the cart kept pushing her cart toward me, giving me little space to move. She loudly sighed behind us.

"Ninety-seven dollars and forty-five cents," the cashier said as Grandma pulled her debit card from her wallet. She looked about to swipe the card, but the cashier stopped her. "We do the chip now," he said.

"What?" Grandma said, not understanding what he meant.

"We. Do. The. Chip. Now," the cashier said, loud and slow. The woman behind me huffed. I squeezed my way past the cart and took the card from Grandma.

"Sorry," I said to the lady behind us as Grandma entered her pin information. The woman had her arms crossed over her chest, but her child with chocolate all over his face smiled at me. Grandma looked angry, but she thanked the man when he gave her the receipt.

She didn't say anything to me until we had loaded everything into the trunk and were seated in the car.

"Why did you apologize to that woman?" she asked me.

"I . . . well, she seemed like she was in a hurry."

"You never apologize for taking up space, Yasaman. You have just as much right to take as much time in that line as you want to," Grandma said.

"Oh, no, that wasn't . . ."

"You don't apologize for who you are. I'm an old lady now and perhaps that doesn't mean much in the world we live in, but I exist and I shouldn't have to be sorry for that. As a woman, you have to know that. Don't ever apologize for who you are," she said.

I nodded and held her hand. It was wrinkled but soft and smaller than mine. I kissed the back of it.

"You're right," I said.

"I'm always right. Tell your mother that," she said. "Now let's go! We have to get to the market before the good vegetables are gone."

. . .

I had spent the past two months on weekends preparing the dishes Grandma taught me to make. My parents were starting to get sick of kuku sabzi, a vegetable herb frittata, though they were pleased to see that my attempts at making it were improving. I had also enjoyed going with Grandma to the ethnic food markets. We went to an Armenian-owned store for fresh and cheap produce and to a Persian bakery for dried barberries and chickpea cookies.

When Grandma would ask where the limoo torshi was at the Armenian grocery, no one would bat an eye, but rather would lead her to the sour dried limes. They had shelves full of items from different countries, all to remind the shoppers of their favorite dishes from places they or their relatives had connection to.

I was doing my best to follow the recipe in Grandma's kitchen.

"Are you sure I can't help you with anything?" Grandma asked. I had spent all day peeling onions and garlic, boiling and stirring rice, and washing vegetables, and I was exhausted. Each dish I made took at least two hours, not including half an hour of prep time. No wonder my parents were fans of ordering takeout.

What I had loved the most about preparing adas polo

(lentil rice), kuku sabzi, and fesenjan (a pomegranate stew) was spending time with Grandma and hearing about how her mother had prepared those meals. And the parties she went to as a kid with her parents and the celebrations she hosted when she raised her own children.

The doorbell rang.

"I'll get it!" I shouted as I tried to beat Grandma to the door. I opened it to find Hannah, wearing a dress and holding a bouquet of flowers.

"I know I'm early," she said. She was never early. She was almost always ten minutes late for everything, which I had factored in for the evening, but she didn't need the extra time. She was wearing a dress I had never seen before. I didn't think she wore anything but jeans and a sweater. Her curly hair was pulled back into a bun. She had taken out her nose ring. Her hand picked at the plastic around the bouquet. Hannah smiled, but there was a look on her face I had never seen before. She was nervous. I didn't think that was a feeling she knew anything about.

"Your timing is perfect," I said as I let her in.

"Do I look okay?" she asked me. I felt the Stay Puft residue bubble up inside me.

"You're perfect too. But you didn't need to, uh . . . You could have come like you usually dress."

"Oh, I'd dress like this if I were visiting my grandma. But she's no longer with us."

"I'm so sorry for your loss," I replied, concerned.

"Oh, no, sorry! I meant she's no longer with us in

Massachusetts! She moved to Florida two years ago," she said. Both of us laughed. I led her to the dining room, where Grandma was already seated.

"Grandma, this is Hannah," I said. I didn't say *my girl-friend,* but I didn't say *friend* either. I hoped that would be a start.

"It's very nice to meet you," Hannah said.

"Hannah! You are so beautiful!" Grandma exclaimed.

"Thank you! So are you," Hannah said. "These are for you," she said, handing her the flowers.

"Oh, thank you," Grandma said as she kissed Hannah on both cheeks, which I had prepped Hannah for. The *thank* sounded like *tank* because the *th* sound was difficult for her to say.

"I can put those in a vase," I said, extending my hands for the flowers. Grandma passed them to me before she sat down again. Hannah sat across from her, and I really wish I had put on some music or something so it wouldn't feel like I was leaving Hannah alone when I brought food in and out of the kitchen.

"Yasaman tells me you are a big fan of *Dancing with the Stars,*" Hannah began. It was the first time I had heard her say my full name. Everyone at school called me Yasi or Big Y, like the New England supermarket chain. Only the assholes called me that, actually.

"Oh! It is the finals! So exciting," Grandma said. I walked into the kitchen to put the flowers in a vase. I could hear Grandma trying to remember the names of the two finalists and Hannah saying she could look up the contestants on her phone. I scooped rice from the pot to a platter. I was grateful that I had plated the other dishes so as not to leave my guests alone for too long. I carried in plate upon plate of food to the dining room.

"There's more?" Hannah exclaimed.

"Hannah, I want to thank you," Grandma said.

"Oh, um, how come?" Hannah said. I could hear her usually confident voice waver.

"Because I think you are the reason my granddaughter learned how to cook!" They both laughed at that. I took a deep breath before I joined them with a dish of kuku sabzi.

"Everything is vegetarian friendly," I said, sitting at the head of the table between Grandma and Hannah. The adas polo, basmati rice with lentils and dates, smelled of butter, ground cinnamon, and sweetness.

"That's my fault," Hannah said.

"Okay. But next time, Yasaman will make you lamb," Grandma said. Hannah looked at me. "I'm joking. You know, like in Greek wedding movie when the husband doesn't eat meat."

Hannah laughed, but I blushed profusely. I couldn't tell if Grandma quite understood how spot on her joke was.

"Befarmaeed sham. Dig in," I said. Hannah looked at me like I was James Bond ordering a martini shaken, not stirred. I guess she'd never heard me speak in Farsi before.

"Hannah, you must come over always," Grandma said as I loaded rice on her plate until she told me to stop.

"I'd like that," Hannah said, placing mint leaves, radishes, and feta cheese on her plate. This was going so much better than I think either of us had anticipated.

"You can tell me who is sending Yasi the texts that make her face red," Grandma said as she bit into the kuku sabzi.

I didn't say anything but just looked at my plate.

"Oh, I . . . I don't know who that could be," Hannah said, not so relaxed anymore. She distracted herself by asking me what was in the fesenjan. I explained it was a walnut pomegranate stew that usually included chicken.

"Now you are red!" Grandma said excitedly to Hannah.

"I am?" Hannah asked in a panic.

"It's all right," I said to Hannah. I touched her shoulder to let her know it was okay.

My grandma noticed. Her eyes widened. I smiled at my grandma and nodded a little to let her know that, yes, this was who made me blush over text messages. Grandma blinked but didn't immediately say anything, which made me worry.

"When I first cooked for your grandfather, I wasn't a very good chef," Grandma explained to me in Farsi. Out of the corner of my eye I noticed Hannah tense up. "But he always lied and said everything I made was delicious when we both knew it wasn't. He said it was delicious because I put so much love into it. Your dinner is good because it was made from love, but you don't need to lie. And neither does she."

I hadn't planned on crying at dinner, but plans changed as my eyes welled up.

"Hannah," my grandma said in English. I turned to

Hannah. She looked petrified. "Yasaman has done a good job, but if you really want delicious food, you are welcome next week."

I wiped my eyes with my palms before I smiled at Hannah. She laughed in relief.

I really hoped Hannah liked Persian food. She was going to be having a lot of it at Grandma's for the foreseeable future.

A STRANGER AT
THE BOCHINCHE

by *Daniel José Older*

Gather, my children, I have a story. This was many years ago, before the Four Corners War, before steel towers devoured the sky, back when Brooklyn's gaslit avenues dipped and curved around great oak trees, and long-necked sauropods loped glumly in the East River, dangling steel rails from their harnesses for the brand-new suspension bridge. These were days of revelry and masquerades burning through the wide-open nights, when we were flickering shadows burgeoning along the dawn streets.

But this story isn't about us, of course. It's about you.

And on this night, a group of you gathered as you always have, night upon night, here at a dim saloon in old Crow Hill called the Bochinche, a few blocks from the penitentiary. And Ramses Garcia Garcia sat in his same spot as always, silent as always, and just seventeen, hands plunking away on the congas, eyes scanning the crowd.

There was a different face amid the revelers this night:
a white face, which was unusual enough at the Bochinche,
but also with large, bulging eyes and tiny beads of sweat
trembling upon his upper lip. The stranger wore a rumpled
pin-striped suit, and an ascot that seemed to clamp the folds
of his fleshy throat. When Oba Ade Iku took the stage to
begin another round of stories, the stranger glared at him,
and Ramses Garcia Garcia glared at the stranger.

Rosie Gene Selwin sat in the crowd that night, and
everyone knew her being there made Ramses play with
that much more fire. Rosie sat just a few tables away from
the stranger. She had her quill out and was jotting down
sketches in a leather-bound tome. Rosie was the inventor
of the crew; most nights she would spend at her regular
table, dreaming up ideas for new machines and weapons to
the strains of that sweet music. During the day you could
find her in the workshop behind the Bochinche, tinkering
and drilling, bringing those dreams to whirring, clanking,
steaming life.

Ramses kept steady time on the congas, a gentle tap-
tapping bolero strut, but his eyes tracked the stranger's every
move. Oba Ade Iku sliced his hand through the smoky air, a
warrior king chopping off his enemies' heads, and launched
into another part of the tale. The stranger scribbled notes on
a scrap of paper, his big eyes glued to Oba.

Ramses glanced at the girl he loved, and then returned to
the stranger. Who was this man? Oba's story reached another
height: the warrior king gazed over the shattered remnants

of an army from his mountaintop. The stranger stood, his teeth clenched, fingers squirming like fattened bloodworms after the rain. Ramses stopped drumming. The stranger reached into his jacket, threw two small packets to the floor. Ramses launched across the stage, spilling the congas to either side.

He bolted toward the stranger just as a billow of smoke unfurled from the ground. The Bochinche began filling with a thick shroud of gray. The stranger ducked past Ramses's swinging arms, dashing toward Rosie Gene. Ramses saw the move, and he hurled toward them as Rosie cracked a bottle across the stranger's face.

The gray smoke thickened. Ramses lost sight of Rosie, the stranger, everything. He pressed forward, shoving through the crowd, feeling for Rosie, coming up short. Nearly overwhelmed by coughing, he found his way outside, stumbled against a wall, and turned toward the masses fleeing the club. Rosie stood beside Oba. "I'm okay," she insisted as Ramses ran up. Ramses hadn't said a word in as long as anyone had known him. Rosie knew how to read the tiny details of his face like it was a language of its own. He started to shake his head. "Stop, Ramses. I'm fine. But . . ."

"That man got away with Rosie's notebook," Oba said. Ramses reeled, caught between good news and bad. That notebook was covered with Rosie's secret designs, pages and pages of mechanical weaponry and flying machines, transporters, intricate technologies Ramses couldn't begin to make sense of. "We have to stop him," Oba said. "I suspect he belongs to the Olritch Scourlings. If they get ahold of Rosie's plans, things may become very dire indeed."

The Olritch Scourlings: an age-old fraternal order that had spent generations trying to open a gateway for their foul gods to worm through into this world. The Scourlings would've been another hilarious cosmic joke if they didn't command such vast wealth. They recruited their brotherhood from the upper echelons of Manhattan's elite, and met in a high-rise downtown that they'd gutted and turned into a shadowy temple. We used to sneak in and laugh at them, rich kids playing silly games, but Oba was right: in the past few years, the Scourlings had taken leaps and bounds toward opening their gateway, and their gods—the Visitors, they called them—were capable of unleashing catastrophe upon us all.

Ramses took Rosie in his arms, kissed her. She whispered a tiny prayer to him: "Take the skies, my love. I'll take the streets," and then turned and hopped on her unimotor. Ramses ducked back into the club as the sound of Rosie's revving engines filled the night. The smoke had mostly cleared out now, and he retrieved his pack.

Fifteen minutes later, he stood before the long, deserted stretch of President Street, strapped up, armed and ready to fly.

The half-moon hung low over Brooklyn tonight, illuminating the shuttered storefronts and a small park. Ramses took a step, then another. Inside him, a tiny list unraveled as he broke into a run: our names, his dead parents and grand-parents, the elders in his spiritual house. He gunned the tiny motor Rosie had pulled from the junk lot. A warm vibration thrummed to life against his back. He leapt once and hit the power charge. Flame exploded from the pack as the me-chanical wings unfolded to either side. The ground fell away. Ramses flew.

Scattered gaslights illuminated the winding Brooklyn streets below. Flatbush Avenue sloped away from the dark trees of Prospect Park. It was four a.m., almost no one out but the night watch and a few straggling drunks. Airships hung just beneath the clouds like great, weightless whales. A mourn-ful horn sounded from the harbor, but otherwise, Ramses's puttering engine was the only noise. He banked northwest toward the bay. Manhattan loomed tall beyond the Brook-lyn clock tower. A single sauropod stretched its long neck out of the dark river: the bridge crews working late. No stranger stalked the streets, though. Almost no one at all.

Ramses swooped low over the tight alley labyrinth of the Harbor District, a clutter of apartment houses squished between the bay and the river. A movement caught his eye and he veered left and cut his engine, gliding along be-tween the dark building fronts. Silence in the streets. Then a clatter of footsteps on cobblestone. There. The stranger stormed along an alleyway and ducked out of sight. A few moments later, Rosie, now on foot, crept along through the shadows after him.

This was back before the bombings; the Brazenvurst Cathedral still reached its twisted spires skyward. Ramses landed on a buttress and waited beside the snarling 'goyles and gnarled saints. Within minutes, the stranger darted from his hiding place and down the cobblestone street. Ramses slid back into the sky, catching a salty updraft from the harbor, and soared through the alleyway and around a corner, following the echoing footfall. The stranger ran into a tenement and slammed the door.

Ramses grinned, eased toward the ground, and landed running. Rosie would be crouched in wait somewhere, preparing. The wings folded back into his pack as he stepped into a dim front room. He took his time on the rickety stairwell. There was no point in showing up out of breath. He let another silent prayer rise inside him, the one said to call on one's warrior spirits before battle, and we gathered in the thick air around him. He unsheathed the machete as he walked into the corridor. At the far end, a single line of light cut the shadows from under a closed door. Ramses walked slowly to it, took a deep breath. And then, with a single kick, he flattened the door and sidestepped in, blade first.

Piles of magazines and ancient books cluttered the tiny room. No stranger. The bathroom, a mildewy disaster, was also empty. A single filth-covered window looked out on the dark sky over the river, the construction lights' glum miasmas in the night. No stranger, but there on the writing desk near the window—Rosie's notebook. Ramses snatched it, threw it in his pouch. Stacks of parchment lay on the desk, messy, ink-blotched writing splattered across page after page.

'Twas two-fold, the insult, Ramses read, *and soon Frederick took it upon himself to find the blasted monstrosity and destroy it, but alas it lurked deep in the Morgath Woods, where its villainous acolytes patrolled and genuflected alongside the hulking, tentaculous mass, inventing stories and casting shells with trembling brown hands.*

Mouth hanging open, Ramses sat. The stranger's story went on, terrifying and achingly familiar, a broken, mutant version of one of Oba's tales: *Frederick huddled in the bushes as the devilish acolytes prepared their sacrifice, grabbing its horns and subjugating it swiftly upon the killing floor. The monstrosity writhed with pleasure, its cackles echoing into the thick swampy night and mixing with desperate mewls from the goat.*

Ramses shook his head, shuffled through the papers. Story after story formed a glimmering, twisted reflection of the tales Oba recited each night at the Bochinche. But these weren't Orishas or ancestral spirits; they were monsters, demons, phantoms of the deep.

Ramses went to stand, but something wet tightened around his ankles. Two greenish, pale tentacles, dripping with thick ichor, had emerged from the underside of the chair and now held each of Ramses's ankles fast against the wooden claw-foot chair legs.

Frantic, he reached for his machete. "Stop!" yelled a voice. The stranger stood in the center of the room. His trembling hand held a revolver at Ramses's face. "Don't move."

The stranger eyed him. "You're the . . . the drummer, aren't you? You've come for the notebook, I presume."

Ramses cold-stared him.

"Well?" the stranger yelled.

The tentacles tightened around Ramses's ankles.

"I don't know anything about it, really. I'm just a writer. I listen. I've been there before, you know, your little club. In disguise, of course. The Scourlings are a benevolent fraternity, mostly. We are curious. The elders sent me, gave me the smoke bombs. They want to know more about you, you know. They think your stories can help usher in the . . . the Visitors."

The Visitors. Ramses looked down at the tentacles that wrapped ever tighter around his legs. Clearly, the stranger's stories had helped him begin to open the portal. That, combined with the technology plans in Rosie's notebook, would allow the Scourlings and their mutant Visitors to rampage through the streets of New York unchecked.

Ramses's fingers were a few centimeters from the machete handle, but then what? He couldn't chop the tentacles away without getting shot. He kept his expression tight, ignored the beads of sweat that trickled down his back.

"The Visitors will come through regardless, yes? We're just here to help them along, really. But you have been here now, you've seen them, the gateway." The stranger nodded at the tentacles. "They like me. I can come and go as I please. But they are upset with you, I'm afraid." The stranger grinned. "Terrible things happen when they're upset." He took a step toward Ramses, gun shaking. "So give us the notebook, yes? And then we'll see if they like you better."

The apartment door swung open; Rosie barged through. The stranger spun around, gun in hand, and in that split second, Ramses Garcia Garcia felt his heart crumble. The girl he loved would be blown away before his eyes, all while trying to save his life. But instead of a gunshot ringing out, the whole world dissolved into a bright white.

The stranger yelled and then something collapsed with a thud. The room was still a pale blur with only the slightest hint of movement in its midst. But Ramses could smell Rosie's perfume and then he felt her climb onto his lap. Her flash cannon. Of course.

"Stop!" the stranger yelled from somewhere on the floor.

"You have my notebook?" Rosie whispered.

Ramses nodded, barely suppressing his smile. He knew what to do.

"Then let's go," Rosie said, clutching him tightly.

Ramses leaned forward and slammed back against the chair, tipping it toward the window, and then clicked the ignition boost on his jet pack.

"No!" the stranger yelled, but his howl was cut short by the roaring engine and then the shattering of glass.

"Ay, m'ijo," Ramses's abuela used to say, her breath thick with tobacco. "Never leave a place the same way you enter."

Ramses thought of these words as he and Rosie exploded through the window and out into the midnight sky over the East River. His vision gradually returned, and the dark city came to life around him. Up, up, up they surged, the chair trailing beneath him as tentacles clenched and squirmed against his legs. Flames danced along the wall of the tenement. He caught a glimpse of the stranger's bulging eyes staring out at him before smoke engulfed the whole facade. He handed his machete to Rosie. She held tight to him with one hand, and with the other she hacked once, twice, then three times at the seething tentacle. It screeched, squirted ichor from its gashes, and then released. The chair tumbled for an instant through open sky, and then a sauropod's gigantic head rose to meet it, mouth open. The chair disappeared with the snapping of those great jaws. The beast paused, its huge eyes wide and then, as if in slow motion, its neck seemed to become boneless. It crashed into the dark waters of the East River and vanished.

"A close one," Rosie said, surveying the city around them.

Ramses nodded, watched the plume of smoke rise toward the stars.

"If they had gotten those designs . . ."

Another nod.

The still-dark world around them seemed to be quietly careening toward some unknown catastrophe. They sensed the coming war, could almost smell it, felt their hidden enemies churning in the shadows. But they knew we moved with them as well, felt our strength and the wisdom of the ages course through them. There would be turmoil and strife ahead, but there would also be stories and music; many long, joyful nights at the Bochinche awaited them, and there were still so many new machines to invent.

Ramses and Rosie held each other close and hurtled through the sky toward Brooklyn.

A BOY'S DUTY

by Sharon G. Flake

When World War II broke out, folks around here signed up right off. I was too young to join. My father was too old. But that didn't keep us from warring with one another. Or me from running away from home six times by my twelfth birthday—the last time for good.

Truth is, I wasn't suited to live on a farm. My father blamed my teachers for my discontent. He ought to have blamed himself. Slaughtering pigs and wringing chicken necks did as much to chase me toward books as any teacher ever did. But it was my father's binoculars and the almanac that pulled me away from the farm first. It's how I got the notion I wanted to be a mapmaker, plotting out every planet and star in the sky. Four years later, I'm sitting at the Lucky Linda Café, homeless. My father would say he could have predicted this.

"Boy! You boy!" yells Mr. Jackson. "Get up. This ain't no flophouse to sleep in day and night."

I keep my head down, plus one eye open because Mr. Jackson is not like his wife, Ma Susie. He wants you to buy your meal, eat it, and be gone. This is a twenty-four-hour café. Some of us have been here since midnight, so he ought to expect a little sleeping to get done.

The café is small. Maybe it holds fifty folks, I'm not sure. I've never seen it more than half-full. I used to sit at the lunch counter across the room. It faces a mirror long as the wall. Sitting here near the window suits me better. My presence doesn't suit Mr. Jackson at all. He looks at his watch. Then looks at it again for good measure. "I got here five thirty this morning. You been asleep at this table the whole time. I can't earn no money with customers doing that."

I sit up, knowing full well this isn't how he treats the other customers. They get served coffee at the regular price. "I paid for my coffee. Two cents extra, like always. And I gave her the tip." It's not true, but his wife nods like it is. One day it will be. Next week I'm signing up with the navy at the recruitment center across the street. I figure I'm plenty old enough, not that Uncle Sam or my father would agree. Uncle Sam says I need to be seventeen. My father thinks I need to come home.

Pulling spit into his throat, Mr. Jackson shoots it into a rusty can. "Country boy here, taking advantage, like they all do," he says to Ma Susie.

I rise up inside and out, yelling. "The sign says buy a cup of coffee and stay and sit as long as you like!" Looking at a few customers looking at me, I lower my voice and settle myself down. "We all came in around the same time, midnight." I'm pointing to the regulars. "He played blackjack. The navy guys played dice." I look left at a man slicing cards faster than a butcher shaving ham. "That one there was drunk before he sat down. You look past it all. Only not when it comes to me."

The drunk man raises his coffee cup, downing the last drop. A sailor with a pretty gal perched on his lap salutes. Another one at the counter hangs his head low while he writes, then cuts his blue eyes at me and smiles. He's been here two whole days. Barely eating. Always writing. His fingers busy, moving a fountain pen from line to line. What is he, sixteen? A liar, maybe, like me. Well, the way Hitler and the Third Reich are fighting, each one of us is needed—Negroes and whites alike. Thieves and liars too, I guess.

Before the Jacksons bought the Lucky Linda Café, it was vacant—a good hiding place for rats and pickpockets on the run. Gutting it, they made it seem brand-new. Mr. Jackson laid the tile floor. Ma Susie made all the curtains by hand. Her brother installed new pipes and put in the lunch counter. A few boys got paid to haul away bricks, broken furniture, and plaster. Mr. Jackson blames me for other things they left with—his wallet, for starters. Now kids aren't allowed much in here anymore. If I hadn't done the mural, I'd be banned too.

"Old man, leave the boy alone." Ma Susie roots around in her apron pocket. "Here's another newspaper article, Zakary

James. I almost forgot." She sits it on the table. "You're famous."

THE BOY WITH HIS EYES ON THE STARS, the headline reads. Planets and stars that I painted on the front and the side of the café fill most of the page. "I told my father. There's more to life than living on a farm."

It was my idea to draw the mural, I told the reporter. I lied about the reason why. Truth is, I was trying to make up for things. The stolen wallet, for sure. I didn't run off with it, but that was just happenstance. I plotted and planned and schemed along with Ezekiel, Randy, Luke, and Tennessee. But they pulled if off without me. One day early. I'd be in the reformatory too, if they hadn't. So, I guess you could say I owe a debt to them.

Painting the mural was like painting a new life for myself. Six months later and I'm brand-new. I wrote that to my father in a letter. I included the article too. He told me to do my duty. To come home and help him run the farm. *Haven't you had enough of the low life?* he wrote. *Of dragging our family name through the mud?*

Ma points to a customer outside in a blue velvet hat. "Her type didn't come in before that mural was painted. Those stars are good advertisement. You see them from the bridge, three blocks over." She pinches my cheek. "We did right, letting you stay."

Mr. Jackson looks at me like I'm the enemy. Then he recalls a boy from a few weeks back who stole the tip jar.

I nearly took off after him. But it's my practice now to

stay clear of boys like myself. Living on the lam, breaking the law, is like drinking rotgut. It only takes one sip to draw you back in. So, I spend my nights at the café. Part of my days here too, reading and painting. When Mr. Jackson has had enough of me, I head for St. Matthew's Church. It's four blocks away. They pay you thirty-five cents a day to scrape the wax off the floors. Sometimes, to keep out of the cold, I do it for free.

Ma wipes crumbs off a table, into her hands. "Nobody's perfect. . . ." She points to the blue-eyed sailor at the counter. "Not him over there," she whispers, "or that poor thing who stole the tip jar." She laughs. "He did stink to high heaven, though." She looks at me. "Negro or white, you boys always do."

Yesterday, she passed along a bar of Ivory soap, a rag for washing myself with, and this shirt. It's a little too tight but it's clean. She lost twin boys to the croup soon as they were born. So mothering every boy who walks through her door gives her pleasure, I believe.

She shakes her head. "He had such pretty black hair. What was he, Italian? Jewish?" Ma Susie asks.

"A thief, like him." Mr. Jackson points to me.

"I never stole anything from you."

He looks at Ma. He pours water into a glass and takes a long drink. Then he brings up his wallet. He thinks he saw one of the boys who stole it. "Susie made me doubt myself, though."

"You're sixty, old with bad eyes," she reminds him. "All these boys look alike to you."

His eyes always find me well enough. "He was your friend, wasn't he?"

I lie. "No, sir." Looking out the window, I pray Ma Susie is right. Because I've no plans to see Ezekiel and those other boys again. I do what I shouldn't when I'm in their company. And for once I've got my eyes on a bigger life.

"Well, if he comes in here—" Mr. Jackson steps behind the register.

"Put that hatchet away." Ma takes it. "They steal to eat. For shoes." She looks awfully disappointed in him. "Our sons would deserve the same kindness."

"Our boys"—Mr. Jackson fights to untie his apron— "deserve to be here more than some." Pitching it onto the table, he walks out of the store.

The blue-eyed sailor puts down his pen, having watched it all.

Ma pats the apron like it's her husband's back she's soothing. Passing by a guest who has walked in, she crosses the street and sits down beside him. There's a bench in front of the recruitment center. When Mr. Jackson has had enough, that's where he goes. I get his apron and tie it on.

Some people can't imagine that I've ever worked a day in my life. But I'm no slacker. On the farm, I worked eight- and ten-hour days. Milking. Feeding. Planting. Pulling. I hardly carry my own weight here, mainly because Mr. Jackson won't have it. But customers are at the door. And it's just me here to greet them. "Morning. Breakfast? Good. Follow me." Cook is hard of hearing. I yell at him as I pass the kitchen. "Two for breakfast. More to come." Seating the couple at the counter, I take their order. Next, I fill their glasses with ice and water. And inspect the silver before I set it out. Pushing open the kitchen door, I read off the order. "Oatmeal, eggs over easy, toast and jam, times two." It's going to be a busy morning, I see. More people are at the door. I take a peek at Ma. She's holding Mr. Jackson's hand. He's eyeing me, but still not satisfied.

Truckers are Ma Susie's favorites. They order double and triple meals sometimes. And tip good. I lead this one back to the lunch counter too. It's easier on me. No running around the whole café taking orders. "This seat work for you? Good." I sit him next to the blue-eyed sailor. That's not the best idea, I see. The sailor grabs his things and heads for a table near the window. Maybe he wants more privacy— who knows? Who cares? I've no time to dawdle. I'm off to seat more customers. Three, to be exact. Just when I start complaining, Ma Susie and Mr. Jackson walk in. She kisses my cheek. He reminds me that I'm not to work the register. Grumbling, he says he may check my pockets for tips.

"Which he earned." Ma stuffs change from a table into my pocket. "And you—apologize," she says to him.

Taking back his apron, he sucks his false teeth. "Sometimes you is worth a plug nickel, I guess."

That's a compliment. One I'll take any day of the week from him.

When the crowd dies down, I eat my fill, with no interfering from him.

. . .

The Lucky Linda Café is thin on customers between noon and three. Which is why I use that time to draw. Years ago, I used loose-leaf paper. But that's too flimsy for a boy on the run. Now I paint on sturdy brown paper, the kind butchers use to wrap raw chicken in. I swiped an entire roll once, and cut it into sheets. Being careful, it lasted me a year. The paintings I drew ended up in the river, though, along with a lady's purse that the cops were determined to retrieve from me.

As carefully as I can, I unroll the paper. It's one solid sheet—ten feet long, to be exact. The best work I've ever done. I modeled the mural outside after it. They're not twins, just in the same family.

"Excuse me." My painting is slipping off the tables. "Can I borrow those?"

The blue-eyed sailor hands me a sugar bowl and salt-shaker to anchor the painting. Standing at attention in his dress whites, he takes his pea cap off. "Jesus. The whole universe." For the first time, I notice blue ink on his fingertips.

My chest puffs. "Counting the Milky Way, there's a thousand stars."

He points to the Big Dipper, Orion's Belt, a meteor's purple tail dragging across the sky. I bring up my favorite planets. "Pluto's the baby of the bunch. That's Saturn—a big show-off. It's got rings. All made of ice and rock. Then rings inside of those. The larger rings are each named for a letter of the alphabet. Know how many of them she has?" I answer before he can speak. "Seven. One day I bet we'll get to the moon. Saturn too."

He doesn't laugh. Like some folks. He looks over my creation. It's done with oil paints and used brushes I won in a crap game. "How long did it take?" he asks.

"Three months for the solar system." I tell him it took two years to do the entire thing. That's not exactly true. I stashed it in the basement of a church for a year. Left it with the pawnshop owner twice. It's tattered at the edges and stained. But people hardly notice.

He reaches out his hand. "Nicholson. Gunner's Mate Jim Nicholson."

He's a tall fellow, I'd say six two or so. I'm just clearing five seven. Blond hair, a skinny nose, he looks as plain an' ordinary as I do. Scared too. Which makes him fit in just fine at the café, even though whites hardly ever come unless they have a Negro girl on their arm or they're down on their luck.

"Zakary James." I shake his hand. "Pleased to meet you." I wipe the sweat from his hands on my pants.

Situating himself at a table, he pulls out a pack of Lucky Strikes and offers me one.

I take two. One to sell to the hobos on Miller Street. The second I'll pass along to the priest at St. Matthew's Church. I never know when I'll need his kindness again. "Shipping off soon?" I pull out my paint tin.

He lights his cigarette and takes a long leisurely drag, but doesn't answer.

"Got a gal? I got a gal. Emma Jean," I lie. I've no time for girls. Not with the life I live. But military men always seem to want to talk theirs up. I'm just making polite conversation.

He's digging through his back pocket and pulls out his wallet. It's black leather, stuffed full of money. "No gal. Just a mother. The best in the world." He kisses her picture after showing it off. Then he gets back to looking worried. "My father was a hero in the First World War. Died some years later."

"Sorry for your loss. I was two months old when my mother passed."

He gives me his condolences. "And *your* father?"

"He never approved of my drawings." I dip my brush in my coffee cup. "Or me."

"My father was hard on me too. Yes, sir. No, sir." He salutes and laughs. "I came to write a letter to him . . . explaining."

"You said *he* was dead."

"He is."

I watch the blinds rise at the enlistment center and use the opportunity to change the subject. "Hope Uncle Sam wears bifocals."

"I am proof that he does." Nicholson laughs.

Ma sits a plate of grits at his elbow. Sliding a forkful of heaven into his mouth, he asks, "Are you planning to enlist? I went in early myself." He leans in and waves me closer. "I wouldn't advise it."

My stomach drops. "Next week. I plan to, um . . . join." I think about my father. He has no use for war, though he served his time. *This is not the Negroes' fight,* he said in his letter. *Your duty is to hearth and home.* I do not mention this to Nicholson.

He finishes the grits in no time. With his hands wiped clean, he shows off his father's medal. "For bravery." Out comes another cigarette. "I joined the navy three years ago, at fourteen. With my mother's blessings. She'll blame herself if I never make it back."

"Well, come back, then."

It's a whole hour before he says another word. Or Ma and Mr. Jackson interfere. They clear tables and wash dishes, serve themselves lunch, and empty the tip jar. I'm painting. Taking advantage of the sun pouring in. Nicholson is back to his writing. It's not long before the tips of his ears turn red in the sun. And he and I are the only customers.

He sets his pen down. "Have you ever seen a torpedo?" *How could I?*

"Oh, the damage they do." He looks at me with pity in his eyes.

For Nicholson's sake, I change the subject. "I noticed you write a lot of letters." Since he came, he's been writing day and night. Filling up the trash can but never the page, it seemed. "I don't care to write much myself. I wrote my father, though. Wish I hadn't is all I can say." I babble on much longer than I would have expected. I'm talking about our farm, the peaches it produces. Some of the sweetest around. City fellows never seem to appreciate such talk. He doesn't either. He looks lost again . . . in his own thoughts. "They say a sailor has a girl in every port. Any truth to that?" I ask.

He fidgets with his pen, dropping it a time or two. "My best friend . . . lost his legs. Both." Using his fingers, he names other boys injured in the war. "Miller, Jamison, McIntyre." Whispering, he starts on the ones who died.

I'm glad when he stops.

"What if it's my turn next? Her time too?"

"Her?" I swallow.

"The *Indianapolis.*"

He looks around. Then whispers. "I don't want to die."

I never think about dying. I can't. I got plans, big ones on the ship and beyond. Not that I share them with folks much. They laugh whenever I do. So, I've learned to lie about those too. To color my dreams small so people feel more comfortable.

I pull a seat over and sit down. "Sometimes it's better to run than fight." I look around the café, as if I don't know it's empty. The soldiers and sailors all gone for now. "Some fellows go AWOL, don't they?"

"Saints alive." Ma Susie looks disappointed in me. "We don't talk like that in here. No, sir." Ma pours coffee in his cup. "We believe in the war effort."

She's in the kitchen when he whispers, "I think about Tahiti."

"What?"

"Tahiti. Where they have island girls. There's no girl prettier on earth." Closing his eyes, he talks about lying in the sun with a coconut drink in his hand.

"Why don't you go?"

"Duty. Duty to my family and country." Sweat from

his forehead drips onto the table. "I came here to write. To apologize to my father for being a coward. I have not found the courage yet." He picks up a notebook and out comes a ticket to Tahiti. "And what about the other boys?" He seems to be talking more to himself than to me. "I have a duty to them as well."

What's a boy's duty to himself? I wonder.

Ma Susie walks in between me and Nicholson. Escorting two military men to their tables, she thanks them for their service. " 'Cause for sure the Negro soldier will put an end to Hitler once and for all. That Jim Crow too." She puts two fingers up on each hand and makes a Double V—the sign for victory at war plus victory over racism here at home—then fills their cups with coffee.

One of the men tips his cap Ma's way. The other cuts his eye toward the door when it opens. In walks a lady with a peacock-colored purse swinging from her wrist. Once she takes a seat, she sits it on the table like a prize.

Nicholson and I resume our conversation. I mention the first teacher I ever lived with. She taught me about the Vikings and Columbus. For the first time, I tell the whole truth. "Ever since, I've wanted to be a sailor. A quartermaster, to be exact. Charting the ship's course, I'll use the stars to guide my way."

"The navy doesn't allow Negroes to do that."

"Not yet. But one day they will. After I'm done, I'll go to school. Then I'll teach astronomy. Maybe at Tuskegee. A colored university. My teacher said that one day, scientists will get us to the moon. I plan to be one of them."

For the first time in two days, he laughs. His eyes tear up. He holds his stomach. Doubling over, he apologizes. As soon as he gains his composure, he bursts out laughing again. Soon sorrow seems to fill his voice. "Tahiti might as well be the moon."

"What?"

"Colored or white, boys like us never follow through, Zakary." He rips the ticket in two. "The ship takes off tomorrow. Duty, right?"

Ma Susie likes to say that the devil is always set to unveil the truth about you. And no sooner than the soldiers leave and Nicholson's words settle in the air does the door blow wide-open—a hurricane of boys rushing in. Four. My old friend Ezekiel among them.

"Heathens!" Mr. Jackson reaches for the hatchet. The woman at table seven reaches for her purse. "Told you all last time—" Losing his temper, he backs into Ma, knocking a pitcher of lemonade out of her hand. "Susie. It's all your fault." With his shirt dripping wet, he takes off running. "Some of these blasted boys can't be saved."

The boys run in every direction. They jump over chairs and boxes, sliding across the floor like ice is underneath their feet. The oldest is younger than me, by a hair. But just as skilled. The tallest is quick-fingered, able to separate people from their wallets in a blink. Like frogs trying to leap out of hot water, they run this way and that, Mr. Jackson behind them but never close enough. "Zakary James. You owe me," he says, stopping to catch his breath. "Fix this!"

Nicholson snatches the youngest one, who kicks and

squirms to be set free. Cook reaches for Ezekiel, but only catches air. I stand where I am, frozen, while Ezekiel scoops the purse off the lady's lap and dances away.

"Zakary James." Ezekiel slows down some. "Catch!"

The peacock purse lands in my hands. The lady stands and gasps. Ma, over by the register, looks sad enough to cry.

"Meet me at the usual place." He flies out the back door, along with the others.

I look across the room and think of all the places I been tossed out of. My fifth-grade teacher's house after he passed on. A friend's place when his folks couldn't feed me any longer. The back room of the library. I stayed there six months, unnoticed. It all comes to an end soon enough, I suppose. Fixing my eyes on my creation, I swallow. Taking pictures of it in my mind's eye, I clutch the purse and almanac and take off running. *Told you so,* I half expect to hear Mr. Jackson say. But like the blues, his words are sad and soft—filled with a bucket of tears. "Zakary James. Stay."

I stop. Everything stops, it seems. "Sorry." I look Ma's way. Then walk out the front door.

•　•　•

We always meet behind the pawnshop on Twelfth Street after we do a job. For the first time, I'm the last to arrive. They probably thought I wouldn't show up. That I'd keep the money for myself.

"What took you so long?" Ezekiel wants to know. He never asks about Luke, the kid left behind. It's how it is. You lose a few along the way. Can't cry over spilled milk.

It's been three hours since I left the café. I spent all that time at the park, thinking. "They sent the cops after me," I lie. "I hid awhile."

Sitting on a trash can, I wave flies away. Then I toss the purse to Ezekiel, who has his fingers shoved deep in one of Ma Susie's peach pies.

"Found two on the back-porch steps, cooling," he says. "Last one. Have a taste."

Passing what's left of it around, he unsnaps the pocket-book. Then thanks me for my assistance. After he counts the money, he offers me the lion's share. It's how we've always done things. The person who takes the biggest risk—gets the biggest reward. Holding out his hand, he waves thirty bucks my way.

"I don't want it."

He faces the back door of the pawnshop. "Get that tele-scope." It's been in the shop window for years. A few times, when the store was open late, I got to use it.

"And keep it where?" I sigh.

Ezekiel hands them each a few bills. The rest get folded and shoved deep in his front pocket. The other boys finish their pie. I take the empty pans and wipe them clean on my pants. "She likes these back." Walking over to Ezekiel, I warn him. "Stay away from them. They're good people."

Ezekiel was the first person I met when I came to this city. I had no coat, or shoes on my feet. At night, I slept on the cold ground. He showed me the ropes. And listened to my stories about the stars and beyond. More than once, I can say. I owe him.

He squats down to tie the younger one's shoe. "Didn't expect you to be at the café. I heard you left town." He stands up. "Wish you had." He looks at the sky. "Is it true?"

"You ask me all the time. Sure, it is."

"The sun is really that far away?"

We all stare up, watching the sun going down. "Ninety-three million miles."

Randy, the youngest one now, sits on the ground, clutching his knees. I watch maggots squirming in water not far away. I look up to the sky. Then I find a stick and show Randy where he can find the Big Dipper, the Great Bear. An hour later, he can name the planet that's farthest away. "Pluto, right?" He smiles.

"Right."

We sit in the alley in the dark, under the lights. Ezekiel rolls dice, eventually winning back most of the money he shared.

"I thought the judge gave you two years," I say to Ezekiel.

"He did." He pulls up his shirt to show me his back. A scar runs from his shoulder to his tailbone. "Sixty-five stitches," he admits.

Put there by a doctor who still needs schooling, I'd say.

"Got it in a knife fight in reformatory. It took three months to heal. I ran off after the doctor took the stitches out." His eyes lose their sparkle when he says, "Wouldn't you?"

I nod. Randy wanders away. They'll spend their money on candy, I bet. Not Ezekiel. He pulls his shirt over his head. "I need a nap." He yawns. "Later we'll go up under the bridge.

I got a pallet there. A blanket for you. Like always." A few minutes later, he's snoring.

I think about my mural. Then I decide not to think about it. I look around the alley instead. The maggots gave up, I see. But the flies haven't. They stick to my sweaty skin. Aim for my lips and ears. I give up on swatting them. And head for the pawnshop. From the sidewalk, I can hear the owner quarreling. A woman wants more money for her pearls than he is offering. The words they use once got my mouth washed out with soap. I step inside, wave at him, and head for the telescope. It's dusty, as usual. But it still works. Not perfectly, though. The lens was always broken. A line passes through the sky when you look through it. I can't see now why I always talked about buying it. Even the knob that makes it turn left to right is rusted.

Stepping outside an hour later, I see leaves get chased up the block by the wind. And the boys get chased out of a store. They run past me laughing. Then dive into the alley, calling Ezekiel's name. A few minutes later, we hear sirens.

I look at the opposite end of the alley and think about making a break for it. Then the fire engines sound. Flying past the alley, it drowns our voices. And gets Ezekiel moving. He talks about not pressing our luck. Taking Seventh Street to Michigan, walking up back alleys, then heading for his place, under the bridge.

I pick up Ma's pans and my almanac, but can't seem to get moving.

"Let's go." Ezekiel slips more candy into his mouth. "They'll be coming for us."

"I dodged the cops," I lie. Ma would never send cops after a boy.

"Somebody's always coming," he says.

"Could be the man from the store up the street. Them reformatory folks, the police." Ezekiel lowers himself to tie Randy's shoes again. "I don't trust nobody." He steps in a maggot puddle. Then leads us out of the alley.

We're on Main Street when I ask for the money he swiped. "A buck. That's all."

"Only a dollar? That's it? It's your loss." He hands it over.

Using a pencil from my pocket, I write down my father's address. "He could use a farmhand. He'll drive you hard. But you'll get paid . . . well. It might work in your favor if you don't mention you know me."

The others fix their eyes on me. I don't know what to tell them. My father's not the type to take a whole crew in.

Ezekiel folds the money neatly. Slides it into his breast pocket. Gives it a little pat, and then squats. He brings up the boy we left behind. "You think Luke's gonna be all right?"

Randy, climbing onto his back, doesn't notice the heavy load.

"Why wouldn't he be? You trained him. Didn't you?"

Ezekiel looks up and down the street and begins walking. I head in the opposite direction.

Scarcely able to keep up with my own feet, I run for miles. Out of breath, I stop at the bridge, blocks away from the café. Looking down, I see pallets and people. Trash cans spitting fire. Crossing the bridge, you can see the café plain as day. Along with a man on a bench. Mr. Jackson, for sure. I take my time getting to him.

"Sit, boy." He has a bat in his hand. I saw him kill a rat with it once.

"I'll stand, sir, if you don't mind." Peering across the street at the café, I see a few of the regulars. "Is Ma Susie here?"

He sounds tired, older than usual. "Sent her home." He leans the bat against the wall. "Of course, she took that blasted boy with her." He takes the pie pans from me. "She don't know, you can never replace what's lost."

I think about Ezekiel replacing me. He can't, I guess. But maybe he doesn't want to.

I sit down and rest on the far edge of the bench. "Maybe she only wants to help boys get back on their feet." I slide in closer. "I plan to join the navy, Mr. Jackson. Go to college. Live my dreams. I have a right to that, don't I?"

He doesn't say a word.

I bring up Nicholson, to clear the air between us mostly. "Did he go with Ma Susie?"

He jumps up. "He better not had!" Then settles himself back on the bench. "Tahiti! Your generation, Negro or white, got sawdust for brains."

Smiling, I think about Nicholson with them girls.

"Quit that smiling. You ruined my day!" He's up now, grabbing the bat.

"I'm sorry. I didn't mean to—"

"Sorry don't always do. What about that woman's money?" he says, bringing up the stolen purse.

"I'll pay it back from my sailor money."

He walks to the curb, prepared to cross the street. "How many years will that take, boy?"

I got no answer for him.

He rubs his shoulder. Crosses the street. Stopping in front of the mural. "Ma made me pay that woman, even for her purse."

"I'm thankful."

"You're indebted to me, that's what you are."

Opening the café door, he asks, "What made you come back? The police coulda been here."

I look at my name written in cursive at the bottom of the mural. "I left things here."

He steps inside first. "You left a mess is what you did. I told Susan, 'I ain't his butler.' You boys. . . ." He grabs a coffee pot. Heading for the kitchen, he talks about making a fresh batch of coffee.

I sit down at my regular table. With my hands behind my head, and my feet up, I stare outside at the moon. A boy's got a duty to hold onto his dreams, I think.

ONE VOICE

A Something In-Between Story

by Melissa de la Cruz

GRAFFITI. The white spray-painted message glowed on the sandstone bricks of Jordan Hall. Couldn't miss it even if I wanted to. A big middle finger and a particularly shocking phrase smack in the middle of my Monday morning, reminding me that—even at what you thought was your prestigious cosmopolitan university, the one you had worked so hard to attend—someone will try to make you feel like you're an imposter. A warning not to get too comfortable. I'll give the tagger this much credit: he or she was bold, choosing this spot, knowing so many students passed through the quad. Even if you didn't see it, gossip was spreading fast.

LAB PARTNERS. My first class that morning? Microbiology. The graduate student running the lab asked us to evaluate different water samples for bacteria. As I prepared a dilution of the sample, my group chatted about what else? The graffiti.

"It's so awful," Yen-Yen said, passing me the pipette.

She had seen a photo of the hate scrawled on the wall.

I placed a drop of the diluted solution onto a Petrifilm plate. We had to wait for the gel to form so we could count bacteria colonies and determine the level of water impurity.

Nate leaned back on his stool. Though his large basketball-player hands tapped out a rhythm on the table, his eyes burned with having dealt with this kind of hate his whole life. "It's business as usual to me." He pulled the hood of his gray sweatshirt off his head. His thick black hair was a frizz from not brushing it before class. "Everyone pretends to be scandalized, but people say racist shit all the time. It's just out in the open now. You think anyone's going to do something about it? Hell no."

Yen-Yen looked up at me with sadness in her eyes. She was expecting me to say something, but I didn't want to have this conversation and couldn't think of anything to say. Despite the difficulty of moving to a new place that was so different from home, I'd gotten comfortable with the brick archways of the campus gates and the crimson flowers filling the flowerbeds. Stanford was a kind of home. But the graffiti had disturbed me in a way I hadn't expected.

Intellectually, I understood I probably wasn't in any sort of physical danger, but I was still unsettled. It compounded this feeling that no matter what I did right, someone was watching, waiting to pull me out of line, throw me in a detention center, then on an airliner with a one-way ticket to the Philippines or wherever.

"What do you think, Jasmine?" Nate had stopped tapping the desk.

"I don't know," I said. "It's not something I was expecting around here."

"It's wild how one thing like that can make you feel so unsafe," Yen-Yen said.

"Words matter as much as actions," I added. "They might only be letters on a wall, but I feel like the graffiti claimed my mental space."

Yen-Yen pulled the film off the dish, revealing red dots of bacteria colonies. "Think they'll find out who did it?"

"Nah," Nate said, marking his notebook, recording the number of bacteria. "I saw them power washing the paint off on my way here. Give it a day—everyone will forget."

"Not me," Yen-Yen said.

I felt conflicted. It might seem weird, but power washing the graffiti so quickly seemed to add to the injustice. It's like the administration wanted to erase the fact that the racist message ever appeared. It's not like I wanted to read those words every day walking to class, but I didn't want the words to simply disappear. I wanted everyone to see the truth—that even Stanford wasn't free from this kind of hate.

SUNDAY NIGHT. Royce and I were out late studying at a friend's house. We walked across campus back to the dorms and slipped through the quad. The graffiti hadn't been

painted yet. I know. I remember gazing at the wall's greenish lights cutting shapes into the darkness. I'd reached for
Royce's hand to get him to slow down a little. We started
talking about how fast the semester seemed to be moving. I
was worried about midterms coming up.

"Microbiology is killing me. I keep mixing up the names
of all the diseases."

"I can help." He snaked his fingers with mine. "Just think
of something that has to do with me for every disease. Crazy
associations help."

"That's a terrible idea," I said, laughing. "I don't want to
think of you and coccidioidomycosis."

"I don't even know what that is."

"Valley fever," I said. "It's a fungal spore that embeds in
your lungs."

"Oh, I can do this," he said. "Coccidio-Royce-o-mycosis.
I'm in your lungs. It works."

"No," I laughed. I've always been able to rely on Royce
to help cheer me up, which I've needed a lot since starting
at Stanford. When I first got to school, I thought the hardest part would be the studying. I'd already been through so
much the last year: discovering my family wasn't documented,
winning a national scholarship I wasn't able to accept because
of my status, fighting through deportation proceedings.

Royce was there through everything. We even talked about
getting married so I could get a green card and be naturalized,
but I didn't want to put that pressure on our relationship. I
wanted America to want me because I was already a part of

the fabric of the country. Not because I would be married to a politician's son.

All of that was only the beginning. I love Stanford, but I've had a hard time adjusting. I'm the first in my family to go to college. Everything my parents have done since our family moved to California from the Philippines has been to make sure I received the best education possible. Whenever I visit them in Los Angeles, I feel like I'm not quite part of the same family anymore. My parents and little brothers are excited for me. They ask questions about everything.

Yet there's still the nagging feeling that I've become a different person. I keep asking myself, "What's my place here at Stanford?"

I was able to push all those thoughts to the back of my mind, until the graffiti appeared on Jordan Hall. It reminded me I'm only living in the United States legally for now. It could quickly change. Something as sudden as a minor shift in government policy can tear families like mine from the dreams they've clung to their entire lives. It's happening all over the country now.

"Try again," Royce said. He hadn't given up trying to make me laugh. "I'm serious. Name another disease."

I squeezed Royce's hand, thinking hard. Impossibly long disease names swam around my head with their confusing multisyllabic letter combinations.

"*Helicobacter pylori,*" I blurted.

"Perfect. 'Helico.' Sounds like a helicopter. 'Pylori.' Kind of sounds like 'pyro,' fire. So I want you to imagine me as a helicopter pilot—except the helicopter is on fire. See? Helicobacter pylori: Royce in a helicopter on fire."

"That was worse than the first one," I said. "But I'll probably use it."

DORM. On Monday night, after my microbiology lab, Royce and I watched a dumb comedy about three high school guys trying to get girls to go on dates with them before graduation. My mind wasn't on the movie. Everything about college life—like fighting with your roommate about over-borrowing her flip-flops, or figuring out whose room is the best place to watch TV—seemed trivial. I turned down the volume and brought up the graffiti again.

"I can't get the image out of my head," I said. "I feel like someone's watching me every time I pass through the quad."

"But that's how they want you to feel." Royce was still half paying attention to the movie. "They might just be some immature frat boys. Don't let them get under your skin. They're probably somewhere laughing about it, thinking they got the whole school up in arms."

"You sure you saw the same graffiti as me?"

Royce paused the movie. "Yeah, I saw. It was really shitty."

"Good. Just checking. Because you don't seem to be nearly as worried."

"They're words. That's all. No one is going to hurt anyone."

"*They're* words?" I echoed. "Where do you think violence starts?"

Royce shrugged. "Just trying to make you feel better."

"I don't want you to make me feel better. I want you to understand how students of color are feeling." I got up from where I was sprawled across the bed. All I wanted to do was leave, but we were watching the movie in my dorm room.

"Why are you making such a big deal about this?" Royce sat on the edge of the bed. He leaned toward me as if he thought a hug would make everything go away.

I wasn't about to be hugged. "Remember when you and I walked back to the dorms Sunday night? How late do you think that was? Midnight? Maybe a little after?"

"I guess. Probably sometime around then. Why?"

"Just play along," I said. "If you'd been walking alone—if I wasn't with you—what do you imagine you'd have been thinking about? I want you to be totally honest."

"I remember being kind of hungry. Maybe I would have been thinking about going to a diner or making ramen. What does that have to do with anything?"

"Exactly." I edged farther away from the bed. It's hard to explain, but I really wanted some space—like being too close to him physically would make me want to stop fighting. And I didn't want to give up this fight. "You know what I would have been thinking about?"

Royce didn't say anything.

"I wouldn't have been thinking about anything except for my safety. I would have been tracking each of those blue emergency phones across the quad, calculating just how far I would have to run to reach one if someone were to attack me."

"Come on, Jas." Royce sighed. "We're at Stanford. What does that have to do with the graffiti?"

"Everything," I say, letting myself out of the room.

JULIA HIGGINS. While leaning over the self-serve bar at the cafeteria to grab some fruit for breakfast, I overheard a couple of girls from another floor in my dorm talking about Julia Higgins. She's a top track star who lives on the other side of my wing. As a sophomore, Julia had already placed third in the 800-meter race at the NCAA Championships. That girl is fierce.

I was expecting the girls to say something about how she might have dumped her boyfriend, or maybe some kind of sorority rush drama. But I nearly dropped a chunk of pineapple into the giant serving bowl of strawberry yogurt when I heard what happened to her.

"They spray-painted her entire car with racial slurs," one girl said. "Does insurance cover that kind of thing? It's going to be super expensive to fix."

"What was on the car?" her friend asked. "I assume . . ."

It wouldn't be hard to guess that Julia is African American based on what the graffiti said, or that the tagging on her car was a lot like the message plastered outside Jordan Hall. A message meant to intimidate students.

Students like Julia. Students like me.

"I don't want to repeat it here," the girl whispered. She glanced to see whether anyone was listening. "I'll tell you later. It was pretty bad."

"I feel so sorry for her," the other said. "I heard people

were taking pictures of her car and sharing them on Snapchat before she even found out."

"That's messed up. Someone should have told her."

"Do you think they picked her at random?"

"I heard she might take a break from the university. She feels targeted."

"Maybe it's just a boyfriend thing. She does have enemies. I bet it's that guy from the wrestling team she dated for a week."

I felt sick to my stomach. Everyone was so concerned with who committed these crimes, but no one seemed to care much about the targets. Just like the administration's order to power wash graffiti off Jordan Hall as quickly as possible bothered me, the students circulating Snapchat photos bothered me too. It had become a sick form of entertainment. Maybe I was being sensitive, but I felt gross when I heard a few students in the dorms making jokes about the hate speech. My stomach churned when a meme started circulating. A line had been crossed.

PRESIDENT ASHBY. It took nearly an entire day for the university administration to respond to the two campus incidents. President Ashby sent an email to all students saying that the incidents on campus weren't representative of Stanford values. At first I felt good about what I was reading. Then I realized that our school president was going to do nothing other than send us all a reassuring email. I wasn't reassured. No one was.

One person's words were never going to make me feel

safe, especially someone like President Ashby, who had never known the kind of discrimination that people of color face every day. Maybe I couldn't stop the graffiti from happening again, but I needed to act on my feelings.

I had to find a way to let other people like me on campus, students who had been discriminated against or were hiding their documentation status, *know* that there were other students who were going through similar experiences and emotions. I needed to show up for them.

And for myself.

AVOIDING MEETINGS. Leaders of various campus cultural groups decided to hold a series of meetings, hinting about a rally. Maybe a march. I thought about showing up to a rally, but I didn't want to draw attention to myself—mainly because of my documentation status. What would Mom and Dad say if I started protesting? Just the thought of it made my head pound.

I imagined Dad standing in front of me.

"Neneng, you'd do this to us? You would go and put a target on your back? They would try to mess up everything around you," he would say angrily. "And don't think they would stop there. Maybe they would spray-paint your brothers' school too. Then what? Our house? They would try to force us out of this country we've fought so hard to stay in."

AT THE GYM. Workout machines buzzed and whooshed. Metal clanked against metal. Royce and I were both sweating on the equipment.

I swear those machines had gotten more difficult over the last year. I'd never stopped working out even though my cheerleading days had come to an end.

We were walking past the free weights when a couple of meatheads lifting weights started laughing. One of them said loud enough for us to hear: "Look at that hot Asian chick."

"They're too stuck-up to go out with me," his buddy added.

Royce was pissed off but didn't say anything to them. Instead, he started complaining at me. "Why do guys do that?"

"It's not my fault," I said. "There's a jerk in every crowd."

"I didn't say anything was your fault."

"It's the way you said it."

"I just mean guys need to cool it."

I felt my cheeks redden. "Do you even know what it's like to be a minority?" I said. "I mean, you're half Mexican, but you look like a white boy, so you don't know how sometimes you just want to hide, blend in, be one of the crowd because you already *are* in the crowd. And let's face it, you don't know what it's like to be a girl." I tried to keep my voice down, but it was difficult. "Before you start acting so overprotective, maybe you should consider what it's like to be me when stupid, shallow guys talk about how they only want to date Asian girls. Or how I feel when someone tells me we all look the same, or how frustrating it is because we're all born to lose. Try playing second banana to the pretty-white-girl standard."

"Jas . . . ," Royce said, trying to shush me.

"I mean, seriously, I could go on, but why? Until you put

yourself in my shoes, you won't be able to understand guys like that outside of your own possessive feelings. No wonder you don't understand the graffiti. You don't think it has anything to do with you."

COME TOGETHER. I could feel myself growing angrier by the day. I'd thought about Dad lecturing me a hundred times. But I just couldn't stay quiet. I found myself fuming every time I thought about the graffiti, the Snapchats, and those gym meatheads. Not to mention, I was very aware of how I'd been lashing out at Royce.

Poor guy was an easy target. You know how those close to you tend to get the brunt of your worst feelings? I knew I had to go to the rally. It was the only place where this kind of anger could even begin to release in a positive way.

Hundreds of students flooded the quad, all to reclaim the space the graffiti briefly tried to inhabit. We needed to cleanse the toxicity that the graffiti had spread across our campus. We were taking back the air, Jordan Hall, the negativity, the oppressive residue that scared so many of us to walk faster with our heads down. We came together through signs of solidarity, songs, chants, poems, food, love, and our mutual strength.

Royce went with me to the quad. He had apologized outside the gym, and though I'd stormed away, he was patient. He knew I needed my space. I needed to claim that space for myself. I also realized that I truly had a place and purpose at Stanford. By all of us coming together to support each other, I discovered my own voice among the voices of others.

It occurred to me, as if a letter slowly slipped through the sky, down past stars, through the dark, and fell into my hands, the words glistening there like their own kind of graffiti scrawled across my heart: We're one voice when we want to be.

PALADIN/SAMURAI

by Gene Luen Yang,
illustrations by Thien Pham

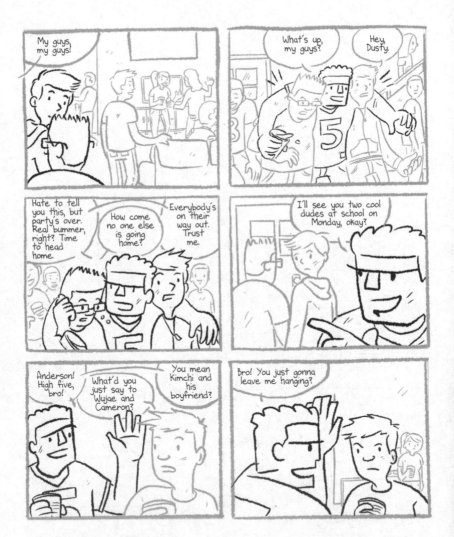

CATCH, PULL, DRIVE

by Schuyler Bailar

My lower back is damp with sweat, but my hands remain cold. My heartbeat quickens as I drive closer to the pool. The parking lot is empty except for Coach's car. It's Monday. I'm the first one to practice, like always.

If I can just make it through the locker rooms and into the pool, I'll be okay. It's half-true. The quiet usually silences everything. But everything could have changed after Saturday night's Facebook post. *Has the entire team read it? What are they thinking? Do they care?* I can't seem to make the move to open the door. My body seems to have another agenda—I remain paralyzed in my seat. The trapped air has gone stale inside the bubble of the car. I pull my hoodie up over my head. I wonder if Coach has already seen me pull in. *Could I leave without him noticing? Can I give up now?*

I just have to get in that water. I run a hand over my chest, feeling the swimsuit underneath. My not-flat chest bulges and I resist the urge to push down the lumps—the remnants of a puberty that never fit. I used to dream of getting breast cancer. Horrible, I know. But then I wouldn't have to explain why I wanted them cut off. I wouldn't have to explain why my body never quite matched my gender.

When I see Parker's car pull around the corner, I frantically open the door and start moving. I don't want to walk in with anyone. That would require too much conversation. I mean, maybe Parker would be okay. He's always been nice to me. We even studied for the PSAT together last fall. But I don't feel like dealing with the questions, even well-intentioned ones. I grab my plain black swim bag and hop down from the truck. Eyes glued to the pavement, I make for the entrance.

As soon as I walk into the building, I'm confronted by two doors: the left marked MEN and the right, WOMEN. I falter, remembering my words from Saturday's post: "And I am proud of who I am. Please refer to me with he/him/his pronouns. . . ."

I can feel Parker's presence behind me, but I hear only my own breath rushing in my ears. The panic is deafening and I want so badly to disappear, into the familiar misery of the women's locker room. But there is no going back: 502 likes on my coming-out status tell me that most of my friends—my entire world—know.

"Hey, Tommy," Parker says. The word *Tommy* glows in my head. This is the first time anyone outside of my family has used my new name. There is no hint of difference in his voice and I find the power to move forward again, pushing open the door on the left. He walks in behind me.

The layout of this locker room is entirely different from the women's. There is only one sink and one stall. There are the urinals, of course. And it smells decidedly worse. I head straight into the stall to pee. Parker stays quiet as several other guys shuffle in behind us. I can see their shoes underneath the bathroom door. My hands revert to their clammy nervousness. *Thank god I've already changed,* I think. *Enough firsts for one day.*

"What's up, cunt?" Roman's voice is obvious. Parker mumbles a response. Roman's pack chuckles at what I imagine is Parker's fear-filled face. I finish and open the door, backpack slung over my shoulder. Everyone falls silent.

"Oh, look, it's our little fag!" The words hit me harder than I had expected and I bend over slightly, feeling all the air leave my body. I look up at Roman, holding back my tears. I say nothing. The locker room seems to freeze for a moment. In the silence, I hear the muffled voices from the pool. *The pool!* Peace. Silence. Disappearance. They pull at me, beckoning, but I resist. *Stand tall,* I tell myself. *Stand tall, even when they hurt you.*

Roman says nothing, and after a few more moments, the staring competition is over.

"Hi, Roman," I say. And leave.

• • •

When the chlorine air rushes into my nose, I relax. The water is perfectly still—no one has broken its surface yet. A few girls are standing at the edge of the pool, reading the workout on the board. I keep my eyes on the concrete deck. I adjust my straps, thankful that this is the last week I'll have to wear the women's suit.

When I look up, I'm face to face with Coach. He nods, not meeting my eyes. My "Hi, Coach" doesn't get a reply. He's not the wordy type. His wiry black hair seems to complement his terse manner. He's over six feet tall and still has the ropey arms and thick thighs of the champion athlete he once was. He's the best coach I've ever had, but I'm terrified of him.

I came out to him about a week ago so that he'd have adjustment time before I told the team—and the world—over Facebook. "You can be whoever you want," he'd said, "but I can't have any distractions on my team.

"None of that rainbow bullshit or you're out." I'd almost laughed—I *was* out! That was the whole point of all this! But I had kept my mouth shut and nodded.

"I just want to swim. This is one of the best programs in the country. I want to keep swimming here." It had taken every ounce of my pride not to cry. He hadn't said much else. With a nearly imperceptible nod, I'd been dismissed.

I wrote him an email later that night, detailing some of the things from our conversation. I'd already started hormone therapy. The mastectomy was scheduled for the end of the month. Six weeks of recovery would allow me to return wearing a men's suit.

• • •

Today, more than ever, I just want to get in the pool. People are staring. Their conversations stop as I walk up.

"Tranny—" The insult is mumbled under his breath, but I know exactly where it came from. No one responds.

I'm the first to dive in. The water rushes to encircle every inch of my body. It fills every curve, every crook, and I feel the tension slip away. As my teammates fade into silence underwater, I relax. Roman's words are gone. Beneath the surface, I am not the girl everyone says I'm supposed to be— in fact, I'm not even sure I'm a person. I'm just swimming. I am a singular action, proof that I am alive and powerful. Under the water, their taunts have no sound. My body has no gender. I am just me.

As I warm up, I slip into the past—summer cannon-ball-diving-board afternoons and old national competitions. I get stuck in a memory of my first travel meet three years ago. Wide-eyed and tiny, I remember staring straight up to see his face. I must have been a third his size. At about eye level, his Olympic rings and Michigan tattoo were peeking out of the top of his Speedo. He had already signed my bright green LONG BEACH GRAND PRIX OF SWIMMING shirt.

I'd awkwardly thanked him and he'd said, "Good luck, little fella." I'd felt a twinge of happiness that was quickly overcome with the familiar shame. I could hear Mom's voice in my head, correcting him: "She's my *daughter*!" I wanted to disappear then, too. I faded into the crowd of people pushing shirts, caps, and papers at him to sign, shouting, "Michael! Michael! Mr. Phelps!" and wandered off to the bathroom. As I approached the door marked WOMEN, I took off my shirt—like I always did—to expose my one-piece women's swimsuit so people could see that I was in the "right" bathroom.

Girls were flowing in and out of the door. When I was only a few steps away, I began to walk more purposefully. I'd learned that pretending I belonged in there made other people more likely to believe it, too.

My entrance stopped the conversation of a group of girls getting dressed around one of the benches. I could tell they were older because they used deodorant. Kids my age hadn't started doing that yet.

I hesitated as I walked toward the stalls, just long enough for one of the girls to get over her confusion. "What are you doing in here? This is the *girls'* room," she had snarled, practically spitting out *girls*. My body flooded with white-water pain—rapids of adrenaline rushing through my veins. I mumbled something, eyes glued to the floor. I decided going to the bathroom wasn't really that important. I bumped into a few other girls who gave me looks of horror as I tried desperately to get to the safety of the pool deck. When the gust of chlorine air smacked me in the face again, I let out a deep breath, exhausted.

It was during those days that I fantasized about digging a hole exactly the shape of my body. I'd lay in the ground, in this hole I'd dug, the earth hugging me tightly from all sides. Time frozen and the world forgotten, I'd lull myself to sleep in this fantasy, the weight of the cool soil holding me as I relaxed into the depths of the earth until I disappeared.

In those days, the water was the closest thing to my fantasy—touching me from all sides, in every way. I would sink into the water, imagining I was fading into nothingness.

• • •

But today, there is no grave-digging. I do not fade. Instead, I am pulled into the water, into myself, and I am undeniably alive. Despite the extra heartbeats, the cold sweats, the unrelenting anxiety, I have found such freedom in declaring my identity to the world. To *my* world. The hiding ends now.

Coach announces the set. It's not too bad, and I'm determined to train harder than ever. *I am still here, fighting!* I want to shout at him.

In his email, he'd said he didn't understand why I'd give up all the success I'd had as a female swimmer. And, if I am honest with myself, I don't have a full explanation: I, too, am grieving my past and potential successes. But he doesn't understand that winning medals can't drive my depression away—that trying to be a girl was killing me.

After we finish the main set, we get up for a few races off the blocks. My suit is tight against my body. It sticks to my breasts and my stomach, reminding me of all the years, all the ways I tried to hide the growing lumps on my chest. Surgery next week, I remind myself.

The boys stare at me as I hop out of the pool and up onto the blocks. I hear Roman's familiar taunt: "Put your elbows together, Chloe. . . ." Not only using my old name, but also demanding to ogle my cleavage. He trails off, adding the last few words under his breath: "Let's see them, faggot." I glance at Coach, wondering if he'll say anything. He doesn't.

"Take your mark—" Coach says instead. "Parker! What are you doing?!" I flinch and stand up from my ready position in time to see Parker fall into the pool. The guys are all snickering. Someone slaps him on the butt as he gets back on the block.

"Scared shitless, Parker? It's just a *girl,*" Roman taunts. "If you don't win, you're a pussy!"

Roman's lips are curled into a smile that's really a snarl. He knows he's pissed me off. I want to punch him just hard enough so he'll remember *I* was the one who knocked him out. But I focus my eyes on the water: *I will not give him what he wants.* I'm ready to show these fools what I can do.

"Go!"

The water crashes over the top of my cap, rushing past my ears. For those few milliseconds, I am alone. It's just me and my cool blue world. Body tightened in a piercing streamline, heart racing to keep up, mind focused only on executing the correct stroke technique. The water is all-encompassing and pure.

Last one, fast one, I hear Coach say in my head. Five or six strokes usually get me across the pool, depending on how tired I am. So the last race of a grueling three-hour practice is probably going to take six.

The speed from my dive lessens, and my surroundings

come into focus. I am no longer alone. I can see Parker in my periphery, and the silence of being underwater breaks as I reach to take the first stroke. I can hear the soft rush of my own wake. I watch my hands grabbing the water and pulling me forward. The top of my head is the first to surface. The water streams over my face as I take my first breath, and though the world is splashing around me, I hear nothing. I revel in this peace—something I haven't felt a lot of recently.

Ever since I fully admitted to myself that I am transgender, fear has tinged almost every thought. Especially anything related to swimming. Only when I learned that I could swim on the men's team—that USA Swimming policy includes transgender athletes—my fear began to fade. Still, I've filled the pool with hidden tears, trying to drown my emotions, terrified of what everyone would think of me—especially in swimming, where gender is so important. Every competition is separated by gender, and boys are normally markedly faster than girls. Competing as a boy could surely mean giving up the medals, the records, the glory of winning. . . .

• • •

After my first stroke, Parker is slightly ahead of me. I've never been great at pullouts. I wonder if I'm already doomed from the start.

As we take the second stroke nearly in unison, heads bobbing up and down at the same time, I try to forget his presence. I don't race well when I let myself get distracted by the swimmers around me. *Control your race, kid; you can't control theirs!* I hear Coach shout in my head. I focus on the water—gliding through it, catching as much of it as I can, and then throwing my arms forward. Sometimes pretending I'm Michael Phelps makes me feel more powerful and I swim faster.

The third stroke slips a bit and my mind wants to give up before my body has even begun to tire. I drag my body forward, repeating what I've told myself a million times: *catch, pull, drive.*

The rhythm returns and my body rushes with adrenaline.

Catch, pull, drive. And I add to the count: four.

Catch, pull, drive. We're nearing the wall. Out of the corner of my eye, I see Parker stretched out, hands already grabbing and beginning to turn. Five.

He has slow turns, I remember.

Catch, pull, drive. Six.

I grab the wall. We turn in sync. As my body switches directions, I relax for a moment. I know I can win.

I can win despite all the boys standing next to the pool deck who've spent the past year making me feel small, making my body feel not my own.

I can win for all the girls who don't understand but who cheer me on anyway.

I can win for my eight-year-old self—for the little boy I have always been, even when I couldn't share him with the world.

I can win.

It doesn't matter that Parker is several inches taller. It doesn't matter that I have not beat him before. It doesn't matter that I'm sick and tired of the name-calling, of being so different, of the exhausting coming-out process. None of that matters. I will win to prove I can.

I know this feeling. It's the feeling I used to have when I was little and we'd go to the skate park. I'd make a deal with my brother not to correct people when they called me his brother. *It's okay,* I'd tell him. *Just let them.* And for a glorious four hours, I was just another skater boy. I was just me.

I welcome this burst of confidence. Pushing off the wall harder than ever before, my body braces in response. My back stiffens in a streamline. I have six strokes left to win.

The swimsuit ripples against my chest, and I wonder how it'll feel to swim unencumbered by breasts—how it'll feel to wear a men's suit and compete against the boys in a real competition, not just in practice.

I take the first stroke off the wall, heading back to the finish, and feel pure power. *Catch, pull, drive.* One.

When I came out to Mom, she hadn't said much. It had been during an offhand conversation about a haircut.

"Mom, I think I'm transgender," I'd said as we drove home from the hair salon. The air was damp with the spring rain, and my long, just-blow-dried hair swept across my face. I'd spent the past hour staring into my reflection as the lady cut an inch, wanting to tell her to chop it all off. I'd continued: "Next time, Mom, I want to cut my hair short, like middle school, like when everyone thought I was a boy." She nodded.

"Okay."

Over the next couple of months, Mom seemed to go over my childhood in her memory, telling me that she should have known. That she should have figured it out.

"Boys' clothes. Boys' soccer team. Boys' haircut. Hating bras . . . ," she'd mumble.

"It's okay, Mom," I'd reassure her. "You didn't have the words. Neither did I."

When I finally got my short haircut Saturday morning, nearly a year after that initial conversation, I'd cried facing the mirror, my reflection feeling more real.

Catch, pull, drive. Two.

I can see Parker's arms out of the side of my eye; I'm slightly ahead of him. Every stroke matters.

Catch, pull, drive. Three.

On Saturday afternoon, I'd sat before my computer screen, my announcement waiting to be posted. The mouse hovered for hours as I played with my short hair. I couldn't bring myself to click Post. When Mom called me down for dinner, I didn't respond. Instead, I remained paralyzed, staring at my words: *"IMPORTANT PSA: Please read."* I'd chosen a new profile picture of me in my favorite button-down shirt, my hair standing straight up from whatever product the hair salon had added. It was the first picture of myself that I'd really liked in a while. It said: Tommy, boy. Tommy, me. Tommy, real.

"Many of you might know this, but this post is to defuse all rumors and half-truths. I am transgender." Even reading the words sent my stomach into spasms. *Was I really about to tell the entire world?*

"Tommy?" Mom stood in the doorway to my room. "Baby, it's dinnertime." I had just burst into tears. And then she was hugging me before I could find a tissue, asking me what was wrong.

What if they hate me? What if my friends stop being my friends? What if I can't stay on my swim team anymore? What if swimming is going to be ruined forever?

Why can't I be normal? Why can't I just be fucking normal?

But the sobs were so violent that all the words just got caught in my throat. She had pulled me over to my bed and sat my non-toddler self on her lap, holding me tightly.

"It's okay, baby, it's okay," she'd cooed as I tried to choke the air into my lungs. Every breath seemed to catch. "Breathe. It's okay—" she'd said again.

"I—I just—what if I can't do it? What if I can't? I can't," I finally burst. "I just wish I was normal."

"Normal is overrated. There is no normal. Stop that," she snapped, returning to her usual manner of tough love. She quickly softened again: "You can do this. And if the team doesn't work, we'll find a new one. You are so strong, baby, you are so st-strong." Her voice broke. She tightened her arms around me and I cried, only now I could feel bits of relief, and safety—maybe a few happy tears, too.

It was another hour before I could press the button. And afterward, Mom took both my computer and phone away so I couldn't obsess over the responses. But I still spent the rest of the weekend drowning in anxiety about today's practice.

Catch, pull, drive. Four. Through the rush of the water, I can hear Roman's shouts. I have no idea what he's saying or who he's cheering on—if anyone—but suddenly the anger is overwhelming. It charges through me. I feel the rage all the way to my fingertips, and I wonder how they're not sizzling in the water. My stomach clenches with body-slacking pain and I see Parker pull ahead of me.

Catch, pull, drive. Five.

Catch, pull . . . but the confidence is quickly draining as I realize I have mere seconds until the race is over. My lungs are demanding air and I feel fatigue seep through me.

There's no point, the darkness says.

NO! something deep inside screams. *NO!*

Looking ahead, I recalculate. I must take an extra stroke if I'm going to have any chance.

But *GIVE UP* pulses in my chest. *NO,* my mind refuses again. *Not for Roman, not for Coach, not for anyone. This is for me.*

Drive. Six.

Catch, pull—

Parker's hands are outstretched, about to touch the wall. I gather all the remaining strength I have to give the hardest kick. *Drive.*

When my head breaks the surface, there is no cheering. I hear only the sounds of us gasping for air. We both turn to look up at Coach, standing in between the blocks with the stopwatch.

Even Roman is silent.

"Tommy, 1:05.8, Parker, 1:05.9—" And I feel everything inside me explode. I can't hold back my grin. Parker sticks out his hand and says, "Good job, Tommy," with a small smile. I take his hand and grin back.

•　•　•

In the locker room, Roman and his friends are already ragging on Parker. "You really are a pussy, letting *her* beat you." The disrespect stings, but I'm madder that this is hurting Parker. He cowers, trying to wash off the soap they keep throwing at him.

I watch as he eventually gives up and starts to put his clothes on.

"Are you a fag, too?" they taunt.

"Shut up, Roman," I hear Parker say through the shirt he's pulling over his head. I have to close my own jaw-dropped mouth this time. In the year that I've been on this team, I've *never* heard Parker respond to any of Roman's jeers. *What is he doing?!*

"SHUT. UP." His head has popped through his shirt and his voice doesn't waver. "Shut up, shut up, SHUT. UP," he says again.

Roman is clearly caught off guard. He's speechless, sporting an astonished look that I've only seen in movies. One of Roman's minions gasps audibly and they all peer at him, then back at Parker. Frantic fury replaces Roman's surprise and he finds his voice: "What—*what* did you say to me?"

"Tommy won. I raced *him* the best I could. Shut up. Leave me the fuck alone." Parker's found courage. I find myself standing up, too.

Roman stutters and strings together nonsensical insults, ending with a final "Faggot."

"You've used that word so many times today," I hear myself say. "Do you know any others?"

What am I doing? Am I out of my mind? Roman whips around, his in-need-of-a-haircut hair falling into his eyes and his "I lift really heavy weights, bro" shoulders hulked forward as if bracing for a fight.

"You don't have much of a vocabulary," I tell him. His eyes flicker with uncertainty.

"You don't have much of a penis," he finally says.

"I don't need one to be me. I'm doing just fine without one, thanks."

Parker's finished getting dressed and I catch him motioning from behind Roman. It's time to go.

"Yeah? Well, next time we'll see how you race against me—"

Parker cuts off Roman's comeback. "Sure, Roman. See ya tomorrow."

Together, we walk out the door.

SUPER HUMAN

by Nicola Yoon

It's when X, the world's one and only superhero, starts to pull off his mask that Syrita realizes that they are all going to die anyway.

It's kind of a relief, really.

Her task to save humanity from destruction is impossible. Everyone knows that. But if X has already made up his mind, then it doesn't matter what she says.

Syrita watches as his gloved fingers hook into the seam of his mask, readying to pull it over his head. The skin of his neck, and then his Adam's apple, comes into view.

"Stop!" she screams, before she can think better of it. Before she can think better of ordering a superhero intent on annihilation to stop doing just exactly as he pleases.

To her surprise, he does stop. His fingers uncurl from beneath the flap of his mask. He tilts his chin up and smooths his hand down his neck. It's a gentle gesture. A pensive one. In that moment, Syrita knows that it's a gesture he repeats often. A part of his ritual for becoming X.

Maybe he puts on black and gray camouflage pants. Next, black athletic socks and black Converse high-top sneakers. After that, a close-fitting, long-sleeved black T-shirt with a big white *X* painted in the center. Black motorcycle gloves are next, until, finally, he gets to the mask.

For this part, he stands in front of a mirror. He gathers both sides of the mask into an accordion fold, raises it to his shaved head, and pulls it down over his face. He does it a little roughly and all in one breath. Afterward, he stands there in front of the mirror, taking a few seconds to adjust. To become. The last thing he does is smooth his hand down his neck.

Watching him now, Syrita wonders if he's making that gesture for the last time. Her fear is evident on her face.

"I won't hurt you," he says. Which is ridiculous, because that is the whole point of her being here.

He is going to hurt everyone.

• • •

Three days ago, X had broadcast his message on all media simultaneously. No one knew how he accomplished that. No one knew how he did anything. In part, the message was as follows:

I no longer believe in humanity. I would see it destroyed. Send someone to convince me otherwise.

After conferring with his counterparts around the world, the president of the United States had called. Syrita was the one they'd chosen. She didn't know what went into the decision-making process—just that the decision had been made. The president had spoken to her for a long time. X had given them three days to pick someone, but they'd come to a decision early so she'd have time to formulate a plan. Save for her mother, no one else was to know that she was the chosen one.

"Why me?" she'd asked him. "Why choose a seventeen-year-old girl? Why not choose a philosopher or a scientist or a religious leader?"

"Because you were the first," the president answered, before the line disconnected.

He meant that Syrita was the first person X had saved the day he introduced himself to the world.

It was two years ago, during one of those car chases that Los Angeles is famous for, and most of what she remembers about X saving her is actually from news footage, in the way that video solidified one's own memories. She was crossing Wilshire Boulevard right in front of the county museum. Through her headphones, she heard helicopters overhead, but that was normal for LA.

Like everyone always said, the accident seemed to happen in slow motion. There was a sound—wheels slipping too fast across asphalt. A smell that reminded her of being a kid and lighting balloons on fire in her backyard. Who could be burning balloons in the middle of the day in the middle of a street? The black Chevy pickup was half a block from her when the police sirens penetrated her music. Finally, she understood what was happening: she was going to die.

But then something lifted her straight up into the air. Not just a few feet, but thirty or forty. She was so high that the truck that was going to kill her seemed small and harmless. She didn't have time to scream or panic. Was she dead? Was this how people actually got to heaven? They shot straight up as if they were on some sort of express elevator? But then she realized she was in someone's arms. He was wearing a mask and his eyes were black and kind and surprised. She remembers thinking how weird it was that he was surprised, because he was the one doing the flying.

After a while he stopped their ascent and they'd hovered in the air for a while. "You okay?" he asked.

How did you even answer a question like that when you're defying physics a few hundred feet in the air?

Still, she wasn't dead. "Yes, thank you," she said.

He flew them down to the ground, but not horizontally like Superman did with Lois Lane in the comics. Instead, they went down vertically as he held her in kind of a hug. After they landed, he flew off to stop the truck by melting the engine and the door handles with his laser eyes. And then he flew away.

After that, the entire world went wild.

At first, people thought it was a meticulous and elaborate hoax, but the sheer volume of cell phone video and pictures persuaded the world otherwise. There was footage of him saving her everywhere.

The *Los Angeles Times* headline the day after he saved her

read: BLACK SUPERMAN SAVES GIRL. The American news out-
lets kept focusing on the section of skin around his eyes that
you could see through the mask. He was definitely black,
they said. One pundit on CNN called him African American, until another pundit pointed out that he was a superhero like Superman and was probably from another planet
and therefore not human, never mind African or American.
Some pundits called him post-racial. Others talked about
race as a social construct, and how interesting it was that it
would take a superhero with brown skin to bring that point
home to white Americans. Other countries ignored the race
discussion entirely, calling them inane. WHY ARE AMERICANS
SO OBSESSED WITH RACE? asked a *Guardian* headline.

Syrita remembers thinking: Isn't everyone?

In the aftermath, Syrita did interviews for weeks with
every media outlet, until her mother put a stop to it. She
spent hour after hour being interviewed by military types.
The frenzy about him never abated: *Who was he? What was
he? Where did he come from? Was he a he? Should we be afraid?*

A few months after he saved Syrita, X sent a note to the
Los Angeles Times telling them that his name was not Superman. It was X. He said nothing about his race.

In the two years since, he became the superhero everyone
expected. He saved people and property across the globe. He
never failed. He was like Superman in every way: noble, with
superstrength, superspeed, and the power of flight.

But then, just recently, everything changed.

At first it was nothing: X didn't show up to a particularly devastating apartment building fire downtown. Maybe

he was on vacation. Did superheroes take vacation? Maybe he had business on his home planet. Maybe he just missed this one. A week later, he didn't rescue passengers on an Amtrak train derailment. After that he wasn't there to stop a mass shooting on a college campus.

Then came the broadcast.

• • •

"Why can't I take my mask off?" X asks her now.

She's sitting across from him at his small dining table in his small apartment.

"You can do anything you want," she says, as if he needed reminding. Despite her best effort, her voice trembles. She'd promised herself she wouldn't let him see her fear.

Beneath his mask, his mouth twists. *Do superheroes smirk?*

Of course he knows she's afraid. He has super senses. Probably he can hear the too-fast rush of her blood pushed along by her too-loud beating heart. Probably he can smell her adrenaline and all the subtle changes in her body that say she's afraid. Probably he knows all the signs of human fear.

"You supposed to convince me," he prompts, leaning back in his chair, arms folded across his chest.

She pulls her shaking hands off the table and clasps them in her lap. Did he really want to be convinced that humanity was worth saving or was this just a game? And if it was a game, then why? Was he bored with being all-powerful?

"You live here?" she asks.

"Expecting something different?"

What *had* she been expecting from a superhero's lair?

Something more like Superman's Fortress of Solitude. Something filled with clear glass crystals and alien technology so impossibly advanced she had no hope of deciphering it. She wasn't expecting this dark, cramped space, overflowing with books and comics. She wasn't expecting the clutter, every surface covered in knickknacks—action figures, Matchbox cars, and Lego pieces. It vaguely reminded her of her younger brother's room.

When she first Googled the address he sent, she'd been surprised at the neighborhood. It was the Crenshaw section of Los Angeles—the kind of neighborhood that white people and rich black people like her mother thought of as dangerous but wasn't.

Through her tears, her mother had asked: "What kind of place is he making you go to?" She hadn't called it a ghetto, but she wanted to. People had strange ways of coping with stress, Syrita reminded herself.

If humanity survived and historians ever got a chance to write about this period in time, they would divide the era into Before X and After X. That's how Syrita felt about herself too. There was the Syrita she'd been before she was almost killed—rich, frivolous, untouchable. And the Syrita she'd become after, was still becoming, really. Still rich, but a little less frivolous. The new Syrita volunteered at a soup kitchen near skid row every month over her mother's objections. The new Syrita said: "It's not a crime to be poor, Mom."

Her mother hadn't responded, just went back to crying.

As per X's instructions, she shared his address with no one else and drove herself over. The drive from her Beverly Hills address to his was like going to another country. The houses got smaller and smaller until they were replaced by cheaply built apartments. Boutique storefronts with designer everything became check-cashing and water-supply places. Cars changed from model-year Mercedes and BMWs to ancient-looking Toyotas and Fords. More people were on the streets—walking or else waiting for buses. Most everyone was black or Mexican. It was the kind of neighborhood that Syrita often drove through on her way to someplace else.

Now, X makes a show of checking out her clothes. "You rich?" he asks.

Syrita frowns. No one has ever asked her that before. Why would they? Almost everyone she knows is rich too.

She shrugs.

Beneath the mask his mouth twists again, but she doesn't think it's a smirk this time.

"Can you tell me why?"

"Why what? Why I want to kill all you people?"

Sometimes, from watching his hero-ing on TV, it was possible to convince yourself that he was human. He looked the part. A human being with some extra bells and whistles. Sometimes, though, his voice would do this thing—double in on itself like it was its own echo—and you remembered. It was too *other* to be human.

That's what his voice was doing now and Syrita couldn't find her own, so she just nodded.

"You really need me to tell you all the ways human beings are shit?"

"You liked us once. You saved us. What changed?"

He has no answer for that, or if he does, he doesn't want to give it. "Why they choose you to talk to me?" he asks.

"I'm the first person you ever saved."

"That was *you*?" He narrows his eyes at her and searches her face. "Yeah, yeah," he says after a moment, recognition in his eyes. "In front of the museum, right?" Syrita nods and he continues, "I thought it was 'cause you're black too." He puts air quotes around the *black*. All at once, he seems defiant and tired.

"But you're not black," she says, remembering the articles from the days after he'd rescued her.

He waves her off as if she'd said something, if not stupid, then definitely naive.

This is not how she thought this would go. Why are they talking about race instead of him ending the world?

She shakes her head and insists, "I'm the first person you saved. I think I'm supposed to remind you of your humanity."

"But I have no humanity. I'm an alien. Like Superman. You didn't hear?" He makes a noise like a laugh, but it is devoid of joy.

And now Syrita knows that X's desire to destroy the world isn't rooted in some existential crisis. Something happened. Something specific.

She pulls her hands from her lap, places them on the table and leans in. "What happened?"

He shrugs. "I got shot," he says.

It's an answer, but not an explanation. X gets shot all the time. There's endless hours of coverage of it. He's in the middle of every fight. Gang shootings. Robberies. Terrorist attacks. The bad guys always shoot at him even though they know he is impervious to bullets. Bullets penetrate his costume but never make it past his skin.

"I don't understand," she says.

"By a cop."

"But why would a cop shoot you?" He is an honorary member of every police force in the country.

He leans forward. His gloved hands are close to hers. Syrita resists the urge to pull away despite her fear.

"I wasn't X when it happened. I was just me."

It takes her a second to figure out what he's saying. He wasn't in his costume. He got shot by the cops for being black on a street.

Syrita doesn't know what to say to that. Television images of protestors marching through the streets of one city or another rise in her mind. They're holding signs that say HANDS UP. DON'T SHOOT. Cops are holding riot shields and batons. It's almost always night. She hears the chatter of news anchors and lawyers and police procedure experts and community advocates all talking at once.

It's not that she ignores these incidents when they happen. It's just that she finds them hard to watch. She doesn't want to know the names of the dead. It's better for her if the details are left vague and the facts are left fuzzy. Because if cops are just killing black men without cause, then how can we all be okay with that? How can she live in a world like that without hating everything and everyone, including herself, for their inaction?

She looks down at her clasped hands. Should she open them? Should she take his hands in hers as a way of offering comfort?

Maybe reading minds is another of his superpowers, because he pulls his hands away from the table and springs to his feet.

Syrita pushes back from the table with such force that her chair topples over.

For the last three days since the president called, the threat to her life has felt abstract—a problem that could be stated and solved with philosophy and words. But now it doesn't. She's never been more aware of her physical body and its breakability.

"Come on," X says, ignoring her fear. "I want to show you something." He walks to the window just behind him and opens it.

She looks from him to the window and back again before realizing that he means for them to leave through it.

"We could use the door," she says, taking a step back.

He doesn't say anything else, just becomes a blur of motion. They're out the window and flying before her brain can register that her feet have left the ground. A few seconds later he sets her down on the roof of the tallest building for a couple of blocks.

She stumbles over her own feet. Human beings were not meant to fly.

"You all right?" he asks, steadying her with a hand on her elbow.

Of course she's not, but she nods anyway.

The morning's fog hasn't yet dissipated, and the pale yellow sun is hazy and indistinct, like it's struggling to come into focus. The air is cool but windless. In the distance, palm trees are still.

X turns his back and walks away from her, toward the edge of the roof. They're about ten stories up.

Some part of her wants to warn him to be careful. Instead she says: "What if someone sees you up here?"

He shrugs and she realizes again that he's already made up his mind about how this will end.

"Know something funny? You fly up high enough, everybody looks the same." He points to the sky. "Black, white, boy, girl, man, woman. Even cops. Just people moving around doing the same dumb shit people always do."

Now he turns away from the ledge and walks back toward her. "Don't last, though. Sooner or later my mind figures out the neighborhood by the type of car or the number of trees or the size of the houses or the number of grocery stores. And once you figure out the neighborhood, you can figure out most of the people. I swear to you. Even the air is different."

He's just a few feet away from her now.

"Tell me about getting shot," she says.

He leans in close, intent on something.

"What you want me to tell?" he asks. "You know this story already. I fit the description of a black kid who did something wrong somewhere in all of America. Don't matter the city. Don't matter the time of day. Don't matter where I was or who I was with or that no way it could've been me. I fit the description. I got stopped. I got shot. No story to tell. You know it already."

"Maybe—"

"Maybe what?" His voice does that thing where it sounds like many voices in one.

She wants what he's saying not to be true even as she knows it is true. She wants to convince him that the cop hadn't meant to do it. The gun misfired because of a glitch. It was a technical accident.

Or maybe X himself had done something wrong, made a move he shouldn't have, didn't put his hands where the cop could see them. It was a procedural accident.

Or maybe he really did fit the description. It was an unfortunate accident. Wrong place. Wrong time.

Or maybe.

Or maybe.

Or maybe.

She knows none of the excuses are true. She knows it in her heart, and where is there to go from here? If she can't convince him the shooting was justified, then his anger is justified. And if his anger is justified, then how can she stop what he wants to do? How can she tell him not to reject a world that has always rejected him? How can she tell him not to destroy the human race?

"I fit all the descriptions," he says.

This time when he starts to pull off his mask, she doesn't stop him.

He hesitates for a moment, and all she sees is the lower half of his face. Dark brown skin. Square chin and jawline. Wide nose, sharp cheekbones. No facial hair. He pulls the mask the rest of the way off. Wide-set black eyes, the most perfect set of eyebrows, bald head. His eyes meet hers and all his parts coalesce. He is beautiful. He even looks like a superhero. If she'd seen him walking down her school hallway, she would've noticed him. She suspects she would've never been able to un-notice him.

The thought doesn't last. He's not in her school hallway. She's not allowed to notice him this way. And those black eyes are looking at her with equal parts pain and wrath. She wants to tell him not to be angry, but how can she ask that of him?

"Don't you ever get tired of it?" he asks her.

He means the constant doubling. He means the awareness of yourself and the awareness of someone else's awareness of you. But not you, your *skin*. One of her white friends had once asked her why black people thought about race so much. "Because you guys do," she had said.

X says, "I'm not from another planet. I'm from *here*. I'm from this neighborhood. My mom made me this way by making a wish. My brother got shot. My uncle got shot. Before she died, my mom said she wanted a world where bullets could never break my skin. The next day, I woke up like this."

. . .

She's come here to convince him not to destroy the world. She's come armed with a litany of human achievements. For every argument, she had prepared a counterargument.

Yes, we are flawed, she had planned on saying. But we have an endless capacity for joy and hope. We are capable of loving unconditionally.

Humans go to war and kill each other.

Counterargument: All wars end and in our peace we find a way to love each other.

Humans invented guns, nuclear devices, torture.

Counterargument: We also invented vaccines, hospitals, prayer.

Humans invented vengeful gods.

Counterargument: Vengeance can be merciful.

Humans invented god.

Counterargument: Or the other way around.

Humans hate what they don't understand.

Counterargument: We are young yet. Give us time.

And so on.

But he *is* human. He knows all this already.

And in the face of this, his justified anger and his grace, she finds that she has no words.

Always the wrong place.

Always the wrong time.

A country that did not value his life.

"What you got?" he asks her now. In his eyes, she sees hurt and anger in equal measure.

It's still not cold and there's still no wind, but she wraps her arms around her body anyway.

"Nothing," she says too soft for him to hear, but he hears it anyway. He's superhuman.

He puts his face in his hands.

His anger is justified and she can't ask him to set it aside. Not when it's his life, his body, that's at stake. If he wants to destroy the world, she won't be the one to stop him.

He says, "They all thought I wasn't human." He presses two fingers into his chest, just above his heart. "But I am."

And finally she knows what to do.

When X got his powers, he didn't choose to destroy. He chose to save.

She's counting on his humanity.

She walks to the edge of the roof and falls backward.

ABOUT THE AUTHORS

Schuyler Bailar is a hapa Korean American, New York City–born Washingtonian. In 2015, he became the first openly transgender man to compete on a Division I NCAA men's team when he was recruited to swim for Harvard University. Schuyler has received widespread accolades for his advocacy and is a prolific public speaker. You can follow his journey on @sb_pinkmantaray (Twitter) and @pinkmantaray (Instagram), or on his website, pinkmantaray.com.

Melissa de la Cruz is the #1 *New York Times,* #1 *Publishers Weekly,* and #1 IndieBound bestselling author of many critically acclaimed and award-winning novels, including the Blue Bloods series, the Descendants series, and *Alex & Eliza,* about Alexander Hamilton and Elizabeth Schuyler's romance. Her more than thirty books have also topped the *USA Today, Wall Street Journal,* and *Los Angeles Times* bestseller lists and have been published in over twenty countries. *Witches of East End*, based on her novel, ran for two seasons on *Lifetime*. *Something in Between* launched the Seventeen imprint at Harlequin Teen. Melissa lives in West Hollywood with her husband and daughter. Discover more about Melissa on Twitter (@MelissadelaCruz), Tumblr (authormelissadelacruz), and Facebook, and on her website, melissa-delacruz.com.

Sara Farizan is the author of the YA novels *If You Could Be Mine*, which won the Lambda Literary Award in 2013 for the LGBT Children's/Young Adult category, and *Tell Me Again How a Crush Should Feel*. The daughter of Iranian immigrants, Sara grew up in Massachusetts and went on to get a BA in film and media studies from American University and an MFA from Lesley University. She lives in Massachusetts. Follow Sara on Twitter at @SaraFarizan.

With millions of books in print, **Sharon G. Flake** has earned an international reputation as a must-read writer for children and young adults. After her 1998 breakout novel, *The Skin I'm In*, she went on to pen ten more books and a play based on *The Skin I'm In*. Sharon's work has been translated into multiple languages and earned numerous accolades, including two Coretta Scott King Honor Awards, a YWCA Racial Justice Award, a Detroit Public Library Outstanding Book of the Year Award, a *Booklist* Editor's Choice Award, and a designation as a Best Book for Young Adult Readers by the American Library Association, among others. But what

Sharon prizes most are the visits she has had with students and the thousands of hugs and letters she has exchanged with them. Learn more about Sharon on Twitter at @sharonflake, on Facebook, or on her website, sharongflake.com.

Eric Gansworth, S·ha-weñ na-sae? (enrolled Onondaga) is a writer and visual artist born and raised at the Tuscarora Nation, and a Lowery Writer-in-Residence at Canisius College. He has also been an NEH Distinguished Visiting Professor at Colgate University. Eric's books include *If I Ever Get Out of Here; Extra Indians,* which earned the American Book Award; and *Mending Skins,* a PEN Oakland/Josephine Miles Literary Award winner. Eric's visual art has been selected for numerous art shows, and he has been widely published in multiple genres. His next YA novel is *Give Me Some Truth.* Learn more about Eric's works on his website, ericgansworth.com.

Lamar Giles writes novels and short stories for teens and adults. He is the author of the Edgar Award nominees *Fake ID* and *Endangered,* as well as the YA novel *Overturned.* He is a founding member of We Need Diverse Books, and resides in Virginia with his wife. Check him out online at lamargiles.com, or follow @LRGiles on Twitter.

Malinda Lo is the author of several young adult novels, including most recently *A Line in the Dark.* Her novel *Ash,* a lesbian retelling of Cinderella, was a finalist for the

William C. Morris YA Debut Award, the Andre Norton Award for YA Science Fiction and Fantasy, and the Mythopoeic Fantasy Award, and was a *Kirkus Reviews* Best Children's and Teen Book of the Year. She has been a three-time finalist for the Lambda Literary Award. Malinda's nonfiction has been published by the *New York Times Book Review,* NPR, *The Huffington Post, The Toast, The Horn Book,* and *AfterEllen.* She lives in Massachusetts with her partner and their dog. Find her on Twitter and Instagram (@malindalo) or at her website, malindalo.com.

A prolific author of fiction, nonfiction, and poetry, **Walter Dean Myers** received every major award in the field of children's literature. He won two Newbery Honors, eleven Coretta Scott King Author Awards and Honors, three National Book Award finalists, and the first Michael L. Printz Award for Excellence in Young Adult Literature. He was the first recipient of the Coretta Scott King–Virginia Hamilton Award for Lifetime Achievement. From 2012 to 2013, he served as the National Ambassador for Young People's Literature with the platform "Reading is not optional." *On a Clear Day, Juba!,* and *Monster: A Graphic Novel* were published posthumously. Myers's full list of works is available at walterdeanmyers.net.

Daniel José Older is the *New York Times* bestselling author of the young adult Shadowshaper Cypher series, the Bone Street Rumba urban fantasy series, and the upcoming middle-grade historical fantasy *The Dactyl Hill Squad.* He won the International Latino Book Award and has been nominated for the *Kirkus* Prize, the Mythopoeic Award, the Locus Award, the Andre Norton Award, and the World Fantasy Award. *Shadowshaper* was named one of *Esquire*'s 80 Books Every Person Should Read. You can find Daniel's thoughts on writing, read dispatches from his decade-long career as an NYC paramedic, and hear his music at danieljoseolder.net, on YouTube, and on Twitter at @djolder.

Thien Pham is a graphic novelist, comic artist, and educator based in Oakland, California. He is the author and illustrator of the graphic novel *Sumo* and did the art for the middle-grade graphic novel *Level Up,* written by Gene Luen Yang, and an ongoing comic strip "I Like Eating," which appears in the *East Bay Express.* Currently Thien is working on his newest graphic novel, *Please, Don't Give Up,* teaching, and eating. A lot. Follow Thien on Twitter at @CobraTalon, and Instagram at @thiendog.

Jason Reynolds is a *New York Times* bestselling author, a National Book Award honoree, a *Kirkus* Prize winner, a Walter Dean Myers Award winner, an NAACP Image Award winner, and a Coretta Scott King honoree. He is on faculty at Lesley University, for the Writing for Young People MFA Program, and currently resides in Washington, D.C. Find Jason on Twitter at @JasonReynolds83 or on his website jasonwritesbooks.com.

About the Authors

Aminah Mae Safi is a writer who explores art, fiction, feminism, and film. Her forthcoming debut novel, *Not the Girls You're Looking For,* is an ode to messy girls, ride-or-die friends, and bad decisions. She has contributed to *& Magazine, Blisstree, Listen Before You Buy* (now *Unrecorded*), *Geek Feminism, Sunset in the Rearview,* and *Tomorrow Magazine.* She lives in Los Angeles with her partner and a cat bent on world domination. Find her on Instagram at @aminahmae and on her website, aminahmae.com.

Gene Luen Yang is currently serving as the National Ambassador for Young People's Literature. His book *American Born Chinese* was the first graphic novel to be nominated for a National Book Award and the first to win the Michael L. Printz Award. It is also an Eisner Award winner. His two-volume graphic novel *Boxers & Saints* was also nominated for the National Book Award and won the *LA Times* Book Prize. Gene currently writes Dark Horse Comics' Avatar: The Last Airbender series and DC Comics' Superman. Secret Coders, his middle-grade graphic novel series with cartoonist Mike Holmes, teaches kids the basics of computer programming. Check out Gene online at geneyang.com and on Twitter at @geneluenyang.

Nicola Yoon is the #1 *New York Times* bestselling author of *Everything, Everything,* which is now a major motion picture, and *The Sun Is Also a Star,* a National Book Award finalist, a Michael L. Printz Honor Book, and a Coretta Scott King

ABOUT WE NEED DIVERSE BOOKS

The We Need Diverse Books™ mission statement—"putting more books featuring diverse characters into the hands of all children"—sounds simple, though it's anything but.

Since 2014, when the organization was founded on the strength of the viral #weneeddiversebooks hashtag, there have been hundreds of thousands of volunteer hours spent attempting to accomplish that mission. We've made great strides in effecting real change, from our mentorship program that allows future diverse writers and illustrators to learn from giants in the field. Our internship program that helps future diverse gatekeepers gain valuable real-world experience inside our industry's top publishing houses and agencies. Our Walter Dean Myers grant that offers much needed financial boosts to creators on the verge of breaking into our seemingly impenetrable industry. The Walter Award, which celebrates the year's shining examples of diverse work. And this book that you hold in your hands.

The inspiration for so much of our efforts, Walter Dean Myers himself, once said, "We need to bring our young people into the fullness of America's promise, and to do that we must rediscover who they are and who we are and be prepared to make the journey with them, whatever it takes. My conceit is that literature can be a small path along that journey."

It is only through the tireless efforts of dedicated young people like you that the face of publishing changes, so we can widen that path that Walter spoke of, and journey toward that American promise together.

There's still work to be done. We hope you'll join us in doing it. Because the mission remains.

Visit diversebooks.org.